Death Vows

MLR PRESS AUTHORS

Featuring a roll call of some of the best writers of gay erotica and mysteries today!

Maura Anderson	Wayne Gunn
Victor J. Banis	J. L. Langley
Laura Baumbach	Josh Lanyon
Sarah Black	William Maltese
Ally Blue	Gary Martine
J. P. Bowie	Jet Mykles
James Buchanan	Luisa Prieto
Dick D	Jardonn Smith
Jason Edding	Richard Stevenson
Angela Fiddler	Claire Thompson
Kimberly Gardner	

Check out titles, both available and forthcoming, at
www.mlrpress.com

A Donald Strachey Mystery

Death Vows

RICHARD STEVENSON

mlrpress

Published by:
MLR Press, LLC
3052 Gaines Waterport Rd.
Albion, NY 14411

Visit ManLoveRomance Press, LLC on the Internet:
www.mlrpress.com

Cover Art by Deana C. Jamroz
Editing by Judith David
Printed in the United States of America.

ISBN# 978-1-934531-33-4

First Edition
2008

This book is dedicated to Pittsfield's bravest.

"We all wear masks."
— *Batman*

CHAPTER ONE

"Mr. Strachey, may I ask, are you licensed to conduct investigations in the state of Massachusetts?"

"I am. New York and Massachusetts have reciprocal agreements on the licensing of private investigators."

"I'm delighted to hear it. I have every reason to believe that you are just the man to help me and Steven out. A dear friend of ours, Bill Moore, is planning to make a horrible blunder. He intends to marry a young man who is plainly not who he says he is, and who we are convinced is up to no good. I take it you are familiar with the rather socially advanced practice of same-sex marriage that the commonwealth of Massachusetts has pioneered?"

The man on my office phone had a voice that sounded as if it was wearing an ascot. Jim Sturdivant had apparently retained the plummy tones long associated with the American WASP upper classes but which now existed mainly in re-runs of eighties nighttime TV soaps.

I said, "My partner, Timothy Callahan, and I would do it ourselves if we lived over there in the Berkshires. Here in New York State we continue to be deprived of the well-known enduring features of legal marriage — adultery, divorce, excess kitchenware, perpetuating the patriarchy, and so on."

There was a pause — Timmy's voice was in the back of my head making little mewing noises over my driving away a potential client — and then Sturdivant said, "Steven and I have not taken the plunge either, much as we would love to. Our nuptials would entail certain family difficulties, which we would much prefer to avoid."

"Like losing a major inheritance, for instance? One of you is waiting for Grams to bite the dust?"

Another pause. Why was I doing this? Maybe because I had worked nonstop through the hot, wet summer on four cases that had been both grueling and decently remunerative. One was the discreet involuntary relocation to Rochester of a blackmailer whose sexual peccadilloes turned out to be even stranger than those of my client, a used-car dealer who liked to hire hustlers in Washington Park, take them home to his garage, and spray them with new-car aroma from an aerosol can. It had been a rigorous July and August, and now, the Tuesday after Labor Day, it would have been lovely to take it easy for a week or so. But why the passive-aggressive needling of this inoffensive man who had called me at the recommendation of a mutual acquaintance?

A patient Jim Sturdivant said, "You are a keen observer of human nature, Mr. Strachey. And — I was warned by Preston Morley — something of a wiseacre."

"Thank you."

"It is not, however, 'Grams' who is the family obstacle. All four of my grandparents have long since passed on. In any event, that's another story. I am most concerned just now about our friend Bill, who is about to marry foolishly. More than foolishly — recklessly, stupidly, self-destructively. None of those terms is putting it too strongly. Barry Fields is a dangerous young man, and Bill is so smitten with him that he is utterly blind to everything but Barry's pleasant personality and physical charms. Which I have to recognize are both appealing, but that is neither here nor there. The man is plainly a cunning fraud."

I had the window propped open with an upended 1985 Albany phone book, and an invigorating cocktail of fresh late-summer air and diesel fumes wafted up from Central Avenue. The mid-morning traffic was heavy but moving in an orderly fashion, and the winos and crack dealers weren't hassling the nice people coming and going at the public radio station across the street.

I said, "What makes you think the guy is a fraud?"

"He tells this story of being from Colorado," Sturdivant said. "But what Barry doesn't know is, Steven has a brother in Denver and knows the state rather well. Barry said he was from Lamar and his father was a corn farmer. But Steven has a nephew in Lamar, which is wheat country. Steven let it go when Barry told the story, but it was the first obvious lie that roused our suspicions."

"Couldn't somebody in that town grow corn too?" I asked. "Timmy's Aunt Moira in Poughkeepsie is well known for her peonies, but she keeps a few petunias."

"There are just too many gaping holes in Barry's story," Sturdivant said. "Such as who his parents are and why they aren't coming to the wedding. First he said they had had a bad year on the farm with the drought out west and they couldn't afford to come. When I offered to fly them here as a wedding gift — a gesture that I must confess was more of a trap than a sincere offer — suddenly Barry's story changed. He said they were too ill to travel. When I asked what their illnesses were, Barry became confused and said he wasn't sure; it was something 'internal.' That's all he could remember, that it was 'internal.' Steven said he was relieved to hear that the senior Fields family members didn't have an external disease."

"He said that to Barry?"

"No, just to me. We've tried not to challenge Barry directly, out of deference to Bill."

"And what does Bill say about these inconsistencies in Barry's bio? I take it you've discussed this with him."

"Well, we've tried," Sturdivant said. "He shrugs it all off. Bill says Barry had a very difficult time with his unsympathetic family when he came out, and it pains him to have to talk about his earlier life. Steven and I both told Bill that reticence is one thing and fabrications are quite another. But Bill is so bedazzled by those red lips and those baby-blue eyes that he is unwilling to see the obvious."

"So Barry is a hot number?"

"He's attractive, and he is also smart and able. He's the assistant manager of the movie theater in Great Barrington, and he's expected to take over when the manager retires next year."

"Barry Fields sounds like a fairly solid citizen to me," I told Sturdivant. "You said he's dangerous. In what way?"

I could hear Sturdivant take a sip of something, maybe his mid-morning latte. My own espresso machine had been out of order for some decades, but I had picked up a cardboard cup of the exceptional brew from the Subway franchise up the block, and I watched two flies carioca around the rim.

"Well," Sturdivant said, "'dangerous' may or may not be going too far. But Steven and I have our well-grounded suspicions. Barry's last boyfriend, Tom Weed, also an older man, died under mysterious circumstances. And I know it's outrageous to think that...The thing is, Tom was wealthy. And his strange death, combined with all of Barry's lies... I guess you can see what I'm getting at."

"Yeah, I see it. How did Weed die?"

"Carbon monoxide poisoning. In his BMW. Three years ago last March, Tom arrived home in Sheffield after a dinner put on by the Supper Club, an agreeable men's potluck group we all belong to. He passed out in his garage with the engine running, supposedly. Barry had worked until nine o'clock that night at the Triplex and was home when Tom arrived around ten-thirty. The question is, why didn't Barry hear Tom drive in, and why did he not check to see what had become of him?"

"A fair question. What's Barry's explanation?"

"He says he dozed off in bed watching *My Favorite Wife* and woke up in the middle of the night with all the lights on. He went downstairs to see what had become of Tom and discovered him dead in the garage. That's Barry's story, at any rate. And the state police bought it."

"Why doubt it? Awful accidents like that happen," I said. "How much had Tom had to drink when he drove home? How far away was the dinner party?"

"About four miles, and I'll make no excuses for Tom in that department. Knowing his drinking habits, I'll admit he probably should not have been behind the wheel of a car. But that is very much beside the point. Barry is a self-described insomniac. He talks about staying up all hours watching Turner Movie Classics. Why did he fall asleep, altogether uncharacteristically, on this particular night?"

"Unless he chose to? Is that what you're saying?"

"It's a terribly harsh suspicion, I know. But Steven and I were not the only people left wondering. The entire Supper Club talked about little else for months afterwards. It was only after it came out that Barry wasn't in Tom's will — as Barry apparently thought he was — that the suspicions subsided."

I said, "And is Barry in Bill Moore's will?"

"Bill has no will. He mentioned this in passing to me once, and when I suggested he make one, Bill sloughed it òff. He is a melancholy man who I think has had some sadness in his life — he's close-mouthed about what it might have been — and an important part of his makeup is a strong strain of fatalism. With no will, of course, Barry Fields will be Bill's sole heir when they marry on September twenty-sixth."

"And Bill is wealthy, too, like Tom Weed?"

"Bill took early retirement from some kind of federal government work — Commerce Department, I think — but there is some family money. I'm not sure how much."

So what was this? Was Sturdivant a meddling buttinsky with an overactive imagination in need of a lecture on manners from Dear Abby? Or could there actually be something dangerous, to use Sturdivant's word, about Barry Fields? It didn't sound that way. But I'd have to know more.

I said, "So what is it you're asking me to do, Mr. Sturdivant? You just want me to check this guy out? See if he's got a past your friend Bill should know about and be either worried or reassured about?"

"Please call me Jim. Yes, that's exactly how you can help. I want to know who Barry Fields really is. And once we know who he is, perhaps we'll know what he is. An uncertain young man with an unhappy past, as Bill has made himself believe, or a conniving con man — or even worse?"

"Jim, I do do background checks for people. Private investigators do this work routinely. It's usually not complicated. But I'm generally hired by the party most directly involved. The ethics here are a little ambiguous. Does Bill Moore know you're asking me to do this?"

Another sip of latte. "No, he does not. Bill is so irrational when it comes to Barry, he might well demand that I call off the sleuthing. But why should Bill's being unaware preclude your taking this on? I would be your client, and I would be the recipient of your report, and it would be up to me to either warn Bill away from Barry, or reassure him, or perhaps say nothing at all."

"I could do this much more efficiently," I said, "with Moore's knowledge and cooperation. And with me nosing around, both of them are likely to find out I'm doing a check on Barry."

"Oh, really? You couldn't do it discreetly? I thought that's one reason people hired private investigators. For their discretion."

This was all new to Sturdivant, who seemed entirely unaccustomed to dealing with persons of my racy calling. "Discretion is possible up to a point," I said. "But inevitably a friend or family member or co-worker gets wind of the snooping and mentions it to the subject. I would not be obliged to reveal your identity as my client. But my not disclosing your identity wouldn't really be fair to Bill or Barry. It would drive them crazy not knowing who was investigating Barry. It's not a position I would want to find myself in, and neither would you, Jim."

He was unfazed by my ethical qualms, which I was trying to find a way around but hadn't yet, and Sturdivant was not helping. He said, "I would certainly make my role known if it seemed necessary, but I seriously doubt it will get that far. One thing I should add, and it may make a difference to you, Don. There are actually two of them — two suspect young men."

"What do you mean?"

"Barry has a cohort who may be in this with him — whatever Barry is up to."

"And who would that be?"

"Bud Radziwill. He's Barry's age, around twenty-seven, and they arrived in the Berkshires together six years ago. They might once have been boyfriends — I'm not sure — and possibly still could be. The two of them are thick as thieves; that I do know. And Bud is as patently phony as Barry is. He tells people he is a 'Kennedy cousin.' He actually goes around announcing that! But, as you no doubt know, Lee Radziwill is Jackie's sister and acquired the Radziwill moniker by marriage to a Polish aristocrat she later divorced. There were two children, a son who died in 1999 and a surviving daughter, Anna. There were no 'Buds' in the Radziwill picture. In any case, it's preposterous to suppose that this fey — ditzy is another word that comes to mind — that this absurd young man is any kind of Kennedy cousin."

I said, "Timothy Callahan once met a Kennedy when Timmy was in the Peace Corps in India. This was some years ago, well before the tables turned and India was busy on the phone instructing Americans on how to make our computers function. Eunice Kennedy Shriver, JFK's sister, visited Timmy at his poultry development project in Andhra Pradesh. He fried her an egg, and she ate it. She told Timmy that a few days earlier Mother Teresa had fixed her an omelet that the nun guaranteed had been made with unfertilized eggs, so there was no chance Mrs. Shriver would inadvertently ingest a tiny fetus."

Sturdivant seemed to ponder this. He said, "Oh, yes. The Peace Corps."

"The farmers Timmy worked with produced unfertilized eggs, too. With so many vegetarians in their customer base, the farmers had to be able to assure everyone that their products contained no meat in any sense."

After a moment, Sturdivant said, "Is this a parable of some kind?"

"No."

"I was beginning to wonder if you were attempting to speak to me in code."

"Nope," I said. "It's just a Kennedy story. It's the only firsthand Kennedy story I've got. You're from Massachusetts, Jim. You've probably got dozens."

He sipped his latte again, or perhaps what I heard was not a sip but a sigh. Sturdivant said, "So I'm getting the impression that you are not interested in pursuing this investigation I have proposed. Our friend Preston alerted me that you pick and choose the cases you take."

One of the flies samba-ing on my coffee cup slipped and fell in. The other one flew off. I said, "You can pick your cases, and your friends can pick their cases, but you can't pick your friends' cases."

"Is this more code-talk?"

"No, just an observation."

"So, you'll not take the case?"

"No," I told him, "I will take the case."

"Oh. Excellent!"

I quoted my terms and Sturdivant accepted them. He told me how to find him in the Berkshires, and where Barry Fields and Bill Moore lived in Great Barrington.

"Don, why have you decided to take this on?" Sturdivant asked. "I had the impression you thought I was overreacting and perhaps a bit of a busybody. But don't you agree that there is at least room for suspicion here?"

"Maybe," I said. "I'll find out, and you can take it from there. But mainly I'm interested in collecting another Kennedy story. Timothy's been dining out on the one we've got for decades now, and it's time we came up with a fresh one. Even if Radziwill is a fraud — escaped embezzler Norman Seffenfeffer from Harrisburg, or whatever — it'll qualify as a Kennedy story, if only a faux-Kennedy story. And those can be replete with meaning about American life also."

Apparently this explanation did not inspire confidence in Sturdivant, who after a moment said, "Well, I'm sure you'll bring your full effort and all of your expertise to the investigation, whatever your interest in the situation."

"You're right. I will."

"Thank you."

We made a plan to meet in Great Barrington for dinner after I made some calls and did some Internet digging, and then rang off.

I phoned Timmy at his desk in Assemblyman Lipshutz's office down the hill at the Capitol. "I won't be home for dinner," I told him. "You're going to have to fix your own octopus *a strascinasali.*"

"Well, I always do."

"I'm dining in the Berkshires with a client. The guy wants a friend's younger male fiancé checked out before they tie the knot later in the month. The client suspects a pecuniary motive, which of course is neither illegal nor unprecedented."

"No, lots of people think I hooked up with you for your four hundred shares of Pennsylvania Railroad."

I explained to Timmy how Barry Fields had raised suspicions about his past with his dubious biography and his murky connection to his last boyfriend's death by carbon monoxide poisoning. I told him, too, that Bill Moore was unaware that I would be investigating the man he apparently loved and was planning to marry, and predictably Timmy didn't like that.

"Why isn't Moore being told? That sounds sneaky and presumptuous."

"Sturdivant thinks Moore is so gaga over Fields — who is some kind of knockout looker and charmer — that he won't even consider criticism of the lad or discuss Fields' possible crass motives. Yes, Sturdivant is going behind his friend's back, but he thinks he has no choice. Moore may have some dough, and once the two marry, Fields will become his sole heir."

"This sounds treacherous, Don. Like some swamp of jealousy and petty intrigue. This Sturdivant sounds less like a concerned friend than a major troublemaker."

"Oh, a swamp of jealousy and intrigue. Timothy, has it slipped your mind what it is I do for a living? There are clients, and there are clients. Anyway, this guy is Hello Kitty next to some of the people whose fees I have accepted over the years."

"And lived to regret a few."

"This is true. There's another angle that's tantalizing, though. Fields has a pal who calls himself a Kennedy cousin. Says his name is Bud Radziwill. Sturdivant thinks Bud the Kennedy Cousin is also a phony, and the two of them are up to something."

Timmy laughed. "Bud Radziwill? Even if he's somehow genuine, he'd have to be a Kennedy cousin eight times removed. I knew a Mario Cuomo staffer once whose name was Alan Kennedy, and whenever he went into a bar he'd tell women he was a Kennedy cousin. Over the years dozens of 'amazing chicks,' as he described them, fell into his arms. He'd always say he had just come from a gathering of the clan at Hyannis Port. And of course what he didn't tell these 'chicks' was, he was a cousin of Wally and Angie Kennedy of Utica."

"Timothy, you have all these Kennedy stories, and I have none. I want to meet this Radziwill guy, and then I'll have a Kennedy story too. I hope you won't mind. JFK was your president, you Peace Corps types. I know you're proprietary about him."

"But, Don, you had your president too — LBJ. And you've got plenty of Johnson stories. Or johnson with a small *J*." He chuckled.

This was an uncharacteristically crude remark from Timmy, and snider than I was used to. I said, "The Vietnamese word for *penis* is *eunice*. Did you know this?"

He laughed and hung up, and I got busy.

CHAPTER TWO

"I think you may have legitimate grounds for suspicion," I told the two men seated across from me at Pearly Gates, Great Barrington's only restaurant with LA-style valet parking. When my aging Nissan had been yanked from my grasp half an hour earlier, my impulse was to yell for the police. The place itself was the color of money, green and black, with gleaming napery and flatwear to which no bits of last night's osso buco adhered. The maitre d' was a bit Paulie Walnuts-like for "America's Premiere Cultural Resort," as the Berkshires had begun advertising themselves in recent seasons. But the overall feel of the place where Jim Sturdivant had suggested we meet was comfortable enough, and my Sam Adams had been well chilled but not to the point of hypothermia.

Sturdivant and his boyfriend, Steven Gaudios, gazed at me with anticipation across the bun basket. Both were tieless, but both wore perfectly rumpled seersucker jackets over soft white shirts of a style that men of a certain class had seen as essential to their presentations of themselves since the fall of Constantinople. In their mid-sixties, Sturdivant and Gaudios were both good-looking, dark-eyed men who seemed to be aging serenely in one of the several ways American money can buy. Their pleasant looks were both of the Mediterranean variety, a surprise in Sturdivant's case, as his voice had suggested more of a Congregationalist background. Neither man had seemed to object to my more functional garb of khakis, T-shirt and leather jacket; this was the Berkshires, where dress codes did exist, even with Edith Wharton's having departed nearly a century earlier, but they were not rigidly enforced.

"So we were right!" Sturdivant said excitedly.

"We knew it!" Gaudios said. "What did you find out? My God, that was quick!"

I explained that while neither Barry Fields nor Bud Radziwill had a criminal record, according to my preliminary inquiries, and that both had satisfactory credit records, neither man had seemed to exist at all prior to their arrival in western Massachusetts six years earlier. Neither had birth records I was able to locate in either Colorado or Massachusetts, or school or early work histories. I told Sturdivant and Gaudios that further Internet and other digging might turn up more recent good or bad information in those two states or others, but the fact that the two men seemed to have been created Adam-and-Steve-like out of the ether just six years previously was in itself a cause for concern.

It was possible, I said, that there was some legitimate reason for their identities being of apparent recent manufacture. It was just barely plausible that they were in the Federal Witness Protection Program, although their youth made that unlikely. They also could have been adopted as teens and changed their last names from something else, though the new identities seemed to have been taken on when the two men were in their early twenties, not several years before. They could, of course, have changed their names for religious or even political reasons, but those types of transformations tended to involve turning from Ed Jones to Ali Hassan Bab-el-Mandeb or Solstice Summerfallwinterspring, not to Barry Fields and Bud Radziwill. And there was also the interesting twist that the two young men's identities apparently emerged at exactly the same moment.

I said, "I was surprised to discover that Bud is actually Radziwill's real name. Bud is usually a nickname, but it's on his driver's license and car registration, it's how he is registered to vote in Great Barrington, and it's the name on his paycheck at Barrington Video. Have either of you ever heard him called anything else?"

"No," Sturdivant said. "He's always just been Bud."

"Or 'Prince,'" Gaudios said and rolled his eyes.

"How does Bud explain his Kennedy connection?" I asked. "People must be interested in that and ask about it."

Now they both rolled their eyes. I was beginning to fear for the integrity of their optic nerves. Sturdivant said, "Well, how *can* he explain it? He can't! He once told me he was related to the Kennedys by marriage, like his 'Aunt Lee,' as he calls her.

When I pressed him, Bud said it was too complicated to explain, but the family didn't make the petty distinctions I was attempting to draw. 'The family'! Can you believe it?"

Gaudios said, "Some of us wondered if Bud might be the illegitimate spawn of Teddy and some West Yarmouth bar girl, but Bud hasn't got Teddy's red nose!" They both haw-hawed over this and sipped their martinis.

I asked if it was certain that Barry and Bud had arrived in the Berkshires together, or if it was possible that they had met in Great Barrington and formed their friendship there.

"Oh no, they showed up together," Sturdivant said and signaled the passing waiter for a refill on his drink. Gaudios gestured at his glass too. "I know they arrived together because they were looking for work, and Tom Weed hired them both to clean out his gutters and do some other jobs around his property. They had an old, red, beat-up pickup truck they drove around. They got a lot of the yard jobs the Mexicans didn't get, because the Mexicans didn't have trucks."

"And the Mexicans probably weren't gay. How out were Barry and Bud?"

"I know Bud flirted with Tom, even though it was Barry that ended up with him," Sturdivant said. "Their gaydar must have picked up on Tom right away, perhaps because he was an antiques dealer in a town where so many of the antiques dealers are gay. These men, many of whom are our friends, don't go around waving the rainbow banner the way the women do. But people in town know who is in bed with whom, believe me."

I said, "And Barry and Bud somehow knew this too. Or quickly scoped out the situation. So, they arrived in town in this old truck?"

"Apparently, yes."

"I don't suppose you recall where it was registered, what state's tags it had on it?"

They thought about this. Gaudios said, "Tom would know. But he's not here to tell us. Tom was a marvelous man. We miss him tremendously. If Barry had just...on that horrible night..." Gaudios squeezed his fist, and the two men looked distraught and angry as they remembered their friend and his slow death in his garage.

The waiter brought me my gazpacho, and my two tablemates their mussels in lime broth and their fresh martinis.

I said, "I'm going to ask around about Barry and Bud as discreetly as I can without letting anyone know who I am and that I'm investigating them. You should know that this may involve a few minor misrepresentations on my part."

I thought that might bring out some squeamishness, but Sturdivant just chuckled. "I had a long, successful career in public relations, Don." He grinned, as if this needed no further explanation.

"It's a black art, I know. The practice of making bullshit exquisite."

Gaudios looked startled. "Jim had many major corporate clients!" He glanced over at Sturdivant, perhaps to see if he was going to slap my face with his lap linen.

But Sturdivant just smiled and said, "A smallish distortion in the service of a larger truth is something I became comfortable with a long time ago."

"Who were your clients?" I said. "Maybe I should be asking for my money back from some of them."

Sturdivant named four Fortune 500 companies which, according to environmental, consumer and human rights groups, were brazen in their regular employment of the Big Lie. I said, "Jim, you're under arrest. Eliot Spitzer is waiting outside with his paddy wagon, and I'd much appreciate it if you would come along with me without making a fuss."

He smiled. "I spent years taking grief from the goo-goo types. The Sierra Club, Consumers Union, all the rest. I knew them all, got along splendidly with most of their people, and wined and dined many of them right here in this very room. But in my retirement, these are the types of people up with which I no longer have to put."

"Right," I said. "Fuck them and the horse in upon which they rode."

Gaudios looked at me in annoyed disbelief. I was disrespecting a man he must have thought of as a great American and who perhaps gave excellent handjobs.

I said, "Tell me about your friend Bill Moore. He retired to the Berkshires from a government job?"

"Bill moved to the area about five years ago from Washington, DC," Sturdivant said. "He's originally from the Midwest somewhere, but he retired here at the suggestion of another federal retiree, Jean Watrous. Jean is a dyke friend of Bill's whose family is from Lee. It was after nine-eleven when a lot of city people with second homes here were moving up permanently or spending long weekends, so real estate was tightening. Bill got here just in time, before the market went through the roof. He's retired, but Bill is not as old as some of us lovelies of a certain age, and he still works part time for a Springfield computer firm. Currently he's helping install a new computer system in the Lenox school system."

I said, "Bill and Jean Watrous are close friends?"

"They play golf together, and we see them eating together at Twenty Railroad, the tavern down the street from here. Sometimes they're with Barry; sometimes it's just the two of them. Jean's ladyfriend, Gwenn, is in Romania teaching journalism for six months, but Jean had to stay behind to look after her elderly mother."

"And what does Jean think of Bill marrying Barry?" I asked.

Sturdivant and Gaudios looked at each other. "There is no way we could possibly know what Jean thinks," Gaudios said. "Jean is not someone who particularly likes men."

"But isn't her good friend Bill Moore a man? I'm confused."

"Well, they have this work connection," Sturdivant said. "But Jean has never been especially fond of Steven and me."

"I'm sure you know the type," Gaudios said, and when I could think of no reply to that, he made what I surmised to be a whinnying sound. Then he and Sturdivant chuckled.

How had I gotten mixed up with these two? Oh, right. Sturdivant was paying me a fat fee. Timmy would be proud that I had not reached over and tipped the two plates of mussels in a lime broth onto their tastefully appointed laps.

I said, "Tell me more about your own friendship with Bill. You're not close enough to him to tell him you've hired me to investigate his boyfriend and not have him object. But you see yourselves as close enough to care greatly about his well-being and to believe that if he were thinking rationally he would appreciate your efforts on his behalf. Can you clarify your relationship? The picture is hazy to me."

"I do believe Bill would describe us as among his closest friends in the Berkshires," Sturdivant said, in a tone that was both defensive and injured. "We met Bill soon after he arrived in the area, at a Supper Club dinner where he hoped to meet other gay men, and we immediately liked him and set out to be as helpful as we possibly could."

"Bill was really terribly alone and forlorn when he arrived here," Gaudios said. "We tried to include him and make him feel welcome, and I have to say that to a considerable degree we succeeded in doing just that."

"When did you see him last?" I said.

They both peered into the pile of mussel shells they had been collecting in a bowl in the center of the table.

"I think last week," Sturdivant said.

Gaudios said, "At the post office, was it?"

"Or at Guido's?"

I said, "Who is Guido?"

"Guido's is the upscale market where we all buy our groceries and wine," Sturdivant said. "It's just south of town. People from Albany drive over here just to shop at Guido's. I'm surprised you don't know it." He looked at me as if I might have had a stick of beef jerky protruding from my breast pocket or from between my teeth.

"And when did you see Moore before that?"

This seemed to stump them. "I'm not sure," Sturdivant said. "Why do you ask?"

What was the deal with these two and Bill Moore? They were seeming less and less like "dear friends" of Moore and more like casual or even distant acquaintances. It was they who seemed to be "up to something," if anybody was. Maybe, I began to think, the way to go here was to do some honest but perfunctory checking up on Fields and Radziwill, write a report, collect my fee, and move on.

I mumbled something about wanting to get a picture of Moore's habits, and then asked, "How did Moore meet Barry? At the Supper Club?"

The eye-rolling this time bordered on the violent. "Oh, my dear!" Gaudios said, and both men guffawed.

"No," Sturdivant said. "Barry was not and is not a member of the Supper Club."

"Why is that? He doesn't eat?"

"It's not a question of eating, but of being eaten," Sturdivant said, and leered with amusement. "No, really," he went on, "Barry did come to dinner as someone's guest a few times, but he chose not to become a member. He was younger than most of us, and I think he just felt a tad out of place. In any event, this was prior to Bill's arrival in the area. I'm not sure where they might have met. Have you any idea, Steven?"

"My God, I think I know!"

"Where? What?"

Gaudios said, "They met at Tom's funeral!"

"Oh, my God!"

"They did. Bill came with Jean, and naturally Barry was there — having just all but murdered poor Tom — and putting on quite a show of grief. What Barry didn't know was, Tom had left everything to his sister in Worthington — this was before marriage was a viable option for gays — and Barry was about to be left homeless. Tom's sister is a vicious bitch, and Barry was ass-over-teakettle out on the street within a week."

I said, "And he moved in with Bill Moore?"

"Not immediately," Sturdivant said. "I think Barry moved in with Bud for a month or two. But Barry and Bill began dating. With Tom barely settled in his grave, everyone commented that it was all in exceptionally poor taste."

The waiter returned and made off with the plate of mussel shells and my empty soup bowl. There were only a few other diners in the room, and the service was brisk, as if to compensate for any delays during the two summer months when Berkshire restaurants were jam-packed with New Yorkers anxious about dealing with the check in order to arrive at Tanglewood or a play or dance performance on time.

I said, "I'm still puzzled."

"About what?" Sturdivant asked.

"About the vague circumstantiality of your suspicions. The state cops were satisfied with the accidental-death story of Tom

Weed's passing. I know a few Massachusetts state homicide investigators, and these people are no dummies. Barry's hooking up with Bill Moore soon after Tom's death is the sort of early remarriage — re-boyfriending in this case — that always sets tongues wagging. But loneliness and emotional need sometimes give decorum a poke in the eye, and usually there's no harm done. I'll go ahead and check further on Barry Fields, if that's what you guys want. His apparent cover-up of his past is unsettling, I grant you that. But I have to tell you, my inclination is to visit Bill Moore and say, 'Hey — what's the deal? Your fiancé seems to have adopted a new identity six years ago. What do you make of that, Bill?' And just see what he says. That approach could introduce an element of clarity into the situation that right now is lacking."

Sturdivant and Gaudios looked at me stonily. Sturdivant said, "But that is not the approach I am paying you to take. It is not the approach you agreed to take."

"It's just a suggestion, Jim. I thought I might try an approach that has a better chance of success than the one I am currently slogging along with."

The efficient waiter, a clean-shaven, hazel-eyed youth clad in the green and black colors of the room, arrived with an assistant in tow, and they placed before each of us plates the size of Soviet tractor discs. Sturdivant's and Gaudios's were each adorned with a morsel of tilapia on a bed of what looked like sea urchin spines, and I got my side of beef and heap o' starches.

Sturdivant remained sulkily mute as we dug in, but after a moment Gaudios said, "You're quite trim, Don, for a man who eats like there's no tomorrow. How do you manage that?"

"Apprehension," I said. "I metabolize much of what I eat into apprehension over what's going to happen next. You won't find this in Atkins or the South Beach diet, but it works for me."

Recovering his corporate-flack mien, Sturdivant said amiably, "I doubt you'll have the opportunity to burn very many calories on this case, Don. Just find out who and what Barry Fields is, and the same for Bud Radziwill, if possible. It's all fairly straightforward, as I see it. Would you please just do that? I'm prepared to offer a bonus of one thousand dollars if you'll just complete this investigation in a straightforward manner and then hand me your report."

My cell phone throbbed against my kidneys. I ignored it and said, "Jim, usually in life you get what you pay for. In this case, I do believe you would be getting something less than what you paid for. However, I'm willing to run a routine check on Fields, ask a few more questions around town, report my findings to you, and then be on my way — no bonus necessary — if that is what you wish to hire me to do."

My cell phone vibrated with a second call just after the first unanswered one, meaning it was Timmy with something that couldn't or shouldn't wait. I excused myself — Sturdivant and Gaudios, predictably getting it backwards, looked at me if this was the height of impertinence — and walked out to the sidewalk in front of the restaurant to take the call.

"I thought you would want to know," Timmy said. "You had a call from Barry Fields, who insists on speaking with you. He sounded pretty upset. He's apparently somewhere near where you are, and he left a number."

"How did he know to call me? He knows already who I am and that I'm checking up on him?"

"He didn't say. He just said it was urgent that you call him. It didn't sound as if he knows you're in Great Barrington now. He just said he needed to speak with you and that you'd know what it was about."

I wrote down the number Fields had left, told Timmy I might be late in getting back to Albany, and reentered Pearly Gates.

I thought it over and then told Sturdivant and Gaudios, "Great Barrington is such a pretty little town. I'm looking forward to spending a few days here."

They both peered at me across their enormous dinner plates, exuding satisfaction.

CHAPTER THREE

"Look, all we need to know is who it was that hired you to check up on us," Fields said. "We have basically nothing to hide, so if you want to drag your ass around town dredging up the boring details of our boring lives, go ahead. Hey, go wild! All we're asking is, just tell us who the fuck it is that is so interested in us that they would actually pay somebody money to track us and find out what we're doing."

"It really is weird and kind of frightening being investigated by somebody," Radziwill added. "It just seems fair that if a person is being put under a microscope by Big Brother, as it were, then that person should be able to find out who this particular Big Brother actually *is*."

We were in Radziwill's apartment in the half-basement of an old frame house up the hill from Great Barrington's downtown. The place was messy and comfortable in a college-apartment way, with wall posters of movie classics — *Duck Soup, Open City, Band of Outsiders* — and stacks of books and DVDs, along with a computer and printer. Simon's Rock College was farther up the hill, so this apartment might have served at times as student housing — though conspicuously missing in post-grad Bud Radziwill's current occupancy were the usual student-decor empty beer cans and ashtray roaches. Like others of his generation, Bud was a clean-living Kennedy cousin.

Radziwill didn't look much like a Kennedy, nor an offshoot of the Polish aristocracy either. He was willowy and wan in his jeans and T-shirt, with an oval face, watery blue eyes, straw-colored hair, and a sizeable tattoo on his right forearm that appeared to be an image of a right forearm with an open hand at the end of it. Fields was similarly dressed, and also light-haired, but sturdier, and with eyes more of an electric blue, and those ample and unnaturally red lips which Jim Sturdivant had noted were a big draw for Bill Moore. I saw why.

Radziwill had nailed me after I did the responsible thing and used my real name and occupation while making inquiries about the two men with a clerk at Southern Berkshire District Court. The clerk, it turned out, was the sister of a man Radziwill had once dated, and she phoned Radziwill as soon as I hung up, and blabbed. Never trust anybody in small towns seemed to be the overly broad and cynical lesson here, though now I was the untrustworthy character in the eyes of my present interrogators. Also, the discretion I had promised Jim Sturdivant was kaput, and I had these two angry young men badgering me to identify the sinister power that was probing into both their lives.

I said, "Unreasonable as it sounds, I cannot divulge to you who my client is. If you hired me, you would insist that your identity be kept confidential. It all has to do with the ethics of my profession."

"Horseshit," Fields said reasonably.

"Not to put too fine a point on it," Radziwill said, "but I do believe it is we who occupy the ethical high ground here. Doesn't your client have to...show probable cause or something before you have the right to start snooping around in innocent people's private lives? Well, not legal probable cause, but just some...*reason* for investigating somebody?"

"In this guy's line of work," Fields said, "the only justification necessary for him to go crashing around in somebody's personal life is a big, fat cash retainer. Isn't that a fact, Don?"

"I'll check the rule book when I get back to my office, Barry, but what you say sounds familiar."

They glared at me. Fields said, "So what are we, under investigation for terrorist activities? Is it that training camp in Afghanistan we went to during our junior year abroad? What set this off, Don?"

"No," I said. "If that was the case, it wouldn't be me; it would be Dick Cheney in here with his battery pack and electrodes. Speaking of junior years abroad, by the way, do you mind if I ask a harmless, non-intrusive, pertinent question? Where did you two go to college?"

Radziwill was draped over an easy chair, but Fields was poised and alert on a metal folding chair across from the sagging couch I was seated on, and he replied without hesitation. "I am certainly providing you with no information whatsoever about myself or anybody else until you tell me who it is who is investigating us and why. And Bud is not telling you anything either, are you, Bud?"

"Nuh uh. I'm certainly not gonna say where I went to college. That's personal data, so to speak." When he pronounced college, it came out *caahhlllege,* and I thought, *Texas — he's from Texas.* Radziwill had lost much of the accent, but there were lingering traces I had been hearing since I had met him, and this clinched it.

I said, "Here's the deal, guys. My client or clients is or are concerned that neither of you seems to have existed in any official record prior to your arrival in the Berkshires six years ago. Give me some plausible benign explanation for this mighty peculiar set of circumstances, and I'll consider naming my client or clients — or at least urge him or her or them to waive the standard confidentiality agreement and give the okay for me to tell you who he or she or they are."

"So there's definitely more than one client," Fields said, sneering. "If there was only one, you would just refer to your 'client.' You wouldn't be talking to us like some pedantic twit. This is quite helpful. We're making steady progress here, Don."

I said, "No, we're not. We're making no progress whatsoever, Barry. Progress would be if you quit trying to change the subject to English usage from your highly suspect non-past. Where *did* you attend college? Where did you go to high school? Who was your kindergarten teacher, and did she sit you on her knee and press your face against her bosom, and did she smell of gardenias? These are questions no person whose past is other than shady would object to answering. But you two refuse to do so. I can only conclude that my clients — yes, there are two or more of them — that my clients are right to have you investigated. And I plan to continue to do so, with or without your cooperation or your opinion of me improving or falling even lower than it is now."

Radziwill said, "So it's our past that your clients are interested in? Not our present?" He looked a little confused by what he seemed to think my answer would be, and Fields looked eager, too, to hear what I might say.

"Past is prologue, somebody once said..."

"Shakespeare," Radziwill put in eagerly, except it came out more like *Shäkespeare.*

"...And it's the continuum of your lives that is going to tell me whether or not you have something to hide, something from the past or the present or both. But I have no picture of a life narrative, in either of your cases, prior to your arrival in Great Barrington, despite my access to a variety of official and semi-official sources that can generally be relied upon to provide basic statistical and demographic information on American lives. Now that's really weird, wouldn't you say?" I didn't mention rural Colorado and the parents with the internal diseases, since I was unsure how many people beyond Sturdivant and Gaudios to whom Fields had told this story.

They looked at each other and then at me. Fields said, "We can't tell you. I understand why there are certain things about our backgrounds that appear bad. Look, can we confide in you?"

"Sure."

"I don't mean confide in you totally. We just can't do that. I mean, can I just admit to you that there are certain things about my life and about Bud's life that are best left unexamined? I'm actually relieved that it's our past you seem the most worried about, and not our present."

"Why? Because you're feeling nervous and guilty about something you're doing at the present time, or are about to do?"

"No," Fields said, "it's because...because today both our lives are an open book. There's nothing for a detective to uncover. I'm actually getting married in a few weeks. To a wonderful man, Bill Moore. I assume you know I'm gay, as is Bud. Everybody around here knows that."

"I was told that, yes." And also about your red lips and radiant blue eyes, now just across the coffee table from me. I reached for an imaginary cigarette.

"So it's really disturbing that at this basically happy time of my life somebody is trying to find a way to fuck things up for me."

"I know you've had some bad luck and sadness in your recent life, Barry. I heard about Tom Weed."

Fields and Radziwill exchanged quick glances.

"What did you hear?" Radziwill asked.

"That you two had been lovers and he died in a carbon monoxide accident in the garage of the house where you both lived."

Fields winced. "Tom and I were not lovers."

"Oh?"

"Tom was forty years older than I am, for chrissakes. We had sex a few times when we first met — his idea, not mine. But basically I looked after his gorgeous house and he let me live there, and we did some social things together. I suppose some people thought we were boyfriends. And Tom probably fed this impression with some people. It was good for his ego, and I knew it and didn't much mind. But when he died his sister inherited the house. The fact that I was not in his will tells you a lot about how close our relationship really was — and wasn't."

"And the sister threw you out soon after Tom died?"

"Margaret was nice about it, actually, despite her discomfort with Tom's being single and gay and the fact that she barely knew me. She said I could stay until the estate was settled and the house went on the market. But because of the way Tom died, I was anxious to get out. Did you hear that he died in the garage while I was upstairs asleep with the TV on, and I woke up too late and found him dead with the engine running and the garage full of fumes?"

"I was told about that."

Radziwill said, "And did you hear that there are people around here who think Barry basically murdered Tom? That he knew all the while that Tom was down in the garage passed out and dying, and Barry was upstairs enjoying *Bringing up Baby*?"

They both watched me. "I heard some people were saying something like that."

"It's not true," Fields said.

"Okay."

"Tom Weed was a sweet man who was terrifically nice to me, and I wouldn't have harmed him for the world. The night he died, I was tired from working a late shift at the theater the night before and then getting up early to meet the plumber who was installing a new pump in the basement. I just conked out while the TV was on, and Tom had had a few too many at a dinner party he went to, and... Life can be unfair and absurd. Death can be too."

"I've seen it happen."

"Luckily, the police saw exactly what happened."

I wondered about that. The state police had ruled the death accidental, which was plausible enough, and there was no real evidence to indicate otherwise. But the police were not in Fields' bedroom to see him nod off while watching a movie. They just took his word for that. Negligent homicide or involuntary manslaughter — the scenarios Sturdivant and Gaudios and their chums hotly chewed over — would have been far-fetched charges for any prosecutor to pursue.

I said, "So where did you go when you left the Weed house with all its unhappy associations?"

"I moved in here with Bud for several months. Luckily he didn't have a roommate at the time."

"And you met Bill Moore soon after Tom died?" At his funeral, for instance?

"I'd known him a little and always liked him, and I found him attractive. But he thought I was Tom's boyfriend and so never showed any interest in me, and I perceived his distance as actually not being interested. But he was interested, and once Tom was out of the picture one thing quickly led to another, and the fireworks were spectacular once they went off."

Fireworks? "You said you were not all that interested in older men romantically. What makes Bill Moore the exception to the rule?"

They both laughed with astonishment. "Bill is no old fart," Radziwill said in his soft drawl. "What Bill is is a hottie. I might choose to be jealous if I didn't have my very own cutie pie to snuggle up to every night."

Fields said, "Josh should be home from work any minute now. You'll meet him."

"But isn't Bill retired? From a Commerce Department job?" I had pictured Moore as resembling a cabinet member for Bush-43 or even Bush-41, if not William McKinley.

Radziwill looked over at Fields, as if this was his designated subject to address. Fields said, "Bill took early retirement. He wanted to get out of DC and have a less high-stress life here in the country. He's only forty-eight and looks ten years younger. That's twenty years between us — but it's not a lot with life expectancies being what they are now."

"Right," I said. "Fifty is the new Prague."

"How old are you, Don?" Radziwill asked. "By the way, we asked a friend in Albany about you. We know you're one of us."

"Oh, you mean an Inuit transvestite? You're certainly resourceful, Bud."

"Our friend said you used to look something like Tom Selleck but that you had outgrown that look."

"It's funny how that works. It happened to Tom Selleck too."

"You look to be around Bill's age," Fields said.

"I am, more or less. If fifty is the new Prague, I'm somewhere between Budapest and Dubrovnik."

Radziwill said, "I have relatives from Crakow. Are you Polish? Strachey sounds English."

"It is. Are you related to Lee Radziwill, by any chance?"

"Yeah, Aunt Lee."

"But you're related, I guess, on the Radziwill side, not the Bouvier side."

"Right. That's why I have cousins in Crakow."

"So, what's it like being that close to the...you know?"

"Do you mean the Kennedys?"

"Yeah."

"I'm not all that close. Oh, we used to go to the compound for holidays, or to Palm Beach. But a lot of those properties have been sold off or turned into museums. It's not the way it used to be. The romance is pretty much gone and the family has drifted apart — as so many large, busy families do after a while."

I was about to suggest that maybe in his next incarnation Radziwill could join a famous family with more current glamour and cachet, the New York Clintons or the Illinois Obamas.

But before I could, Radziwill's boyfriend, Josh, came home from work and ambled in the door. It was the waiter from Pearly Gates. He exclaimed cheerily to Radziwill and Fields, "How did you ever let *this* guy in the door? He's a friend of the toads!"

I knew immediately who "the toads" were, and so, by the way their eyes bugged out, did Radziwill and Fields.

CHAPTER FOUR

"*They* are your clients, aren't they?" Fields said, in a tone and with a look that indicated I had been discovered to be in league with a well-known pair of local necrophiliacs.

"I don't see how you can conclude that, Barry."

"Of course they are! It all adds up. I'm marrying Bill, and Bill owes Jim and Steven money. And they're afraid I'll do to Bill what they enjoy thinking I did to Tom Weed — murder him, literally, or in effect — and I'll get hold of Bill's property, and they'll never get their money back. They want to dig something up on me and scare me off. Or scare Bill off from marrying me. Now I get it! I'm right, aren't I, Don?"

This was getting complicated, though it all had an elegant simplicity to it, too. Fields' description of events so far had a ring of truth to it lacking in Sturdivant's ever increasingly hokey-sounding tale of compassionate concern for his and Gaudios's — the toads — "dear friend" Bill Moore. But there was a large complicating factor in this unfolding saga, and that complicating factor looked more and more as if it was me.

I said, "How come you refer to Jim and Steven as the toads? And in a tone that is, if I'm not mistaken, pejorative?"

Radziwill said, "It's short for 'those poisonous toads.' Not to put too fine a point on it."

"Poisonous in what way?" I asked.

"Poisonous," Fields said, "as in malicious, bitchy, meddling and treacherous. Jim and Steven see themselves as the reigning divas of gay southern Berkshire County. They're both snobs and control freaks."

"And lousy tippers," Josh the waiter/boyfriend added.

"Jim became wealthy collecting stock options from the corporations he flacked for," Fields said. "He's given a lot away to the state Republican Party — he's got a picture on his living-room wall of him standing with an ecstatic Mitt Romney — and locally he donates to respectable but homophobic organizations like the Boy Scouts. Jim also lends money at below-market interest rates to certain friends and acquaintances in need. Except, not everyone is eligible for this service. If you're over forty, you can pretty much forget it — Bill was the only exception to this rule that we know of. And there are conditions attached that only become apparent just before Jim cuts the check for the recipient."

The three looked at me with a queasy expectancy, as if my acquaintanceship with Sturdivant and Gaudios — the precise nature of which they had guessed with no trouble at all — would have clued me in on their idea of any obligatory "condition."

I said, "Is the condition sexual?"

I was making a stab, having eliminated political conditions, spiritual conditions, and astrological conditions. This was based on my investigator's knowledge of how extortion often works once you eliminate cash as the desired currency of exchange.

Radziwill said, "Jim and Steven have a hot tub. You have to get naked and get in it with them."

"Don't forget the dog," Josh put in.

"They have a fluffy white terrier," Radziwill said as the other two watched me react. "You get in the hot tub with Jim and Steven and What-Not. You all drink martinis — the dog has one, too. And then the fun begins. If you want to call it that. I have to say, they do let the dog out before things really get going."

"I'm sure you'd never convince Rick Santorum of that," I said, trying unsuccessfully not to visualize any of this. "But can't people just say no, thank you?"

"You can say that, yes," Fields said. "But if you do — and everybody knows this — then difficulties suddenly arise with the loan. Jim says, oh, by the way, the market has gone south, and my finances are looking dicier than they did last week, and the rate on the loan will have to be half a point above the market rate instead of half a point below. At that point, the loan recipient either shuts his eyes and slides into the tub, or he heads over to Great Barrington Savings Bank to get the best deal he can."

"And Bill Moore...slid in?"

"It's how he got the down payment on his house," Fields said. "Bill has a federal pension, but he left the government with very little in savings. He said the hot-tub experience was icky and humiliating, but it wasn't nearly as bad as some other things he did during his years in Washington that he had no way of avoiding without jeopardizing his career and livelihood."

"Bill's dick was his collateral," Radziwill said. "The loan department won't accept that at Great Barrington Savings Bank, so far as I know."

"Unless you get Arthur Homler as your loan officer," Josh put in, and they all chuckled.

My mind began to force to the surface shameful memories of sex I had had in earlier years for reasons other than love or fun. But I shoved these thoughts back down into their seamy cerebral storage bins. At any rate, Bill Moore seemed to be beyond an age where he would be willing to make his body available in exchange for mere money, or would even be requested to do so, no matter how humpy a forty-eight-year-old he was. Fields seemed to suggest, and perhaps this was the answer, that Moore was a man who had known deep shame previously and was more prepared than some men would be to degrade himself. Of course, another plausible explanation was, a blowjob is only a blowjob — if in fact that's what we were talking about here.

I said, "How much does Bill owe the toads?"

"It's down to around thirty-four thousand three hundred," Fields said. "It was forty, but the front end is mostly interest. Just like it is with the banks."

"And you think Sturdivant and Gaudios see you and your marriage to Bill as a threat to their recovering their loan?"

Radziwill said, "Barry is *sooooo* dangerous, doncha know? After all, he killed Tom Weed, didn't he? And Jim and Steven know Barry can barely stand them. Not to put too fine a point on it." More Texas inflections.

"Bill must not be too crazy about Jim and Steven either," I said.

"He despises them."

This was Jim Sturdivant's "dear friend" Fields was speaking of. So it was true. I had been had. But where to go from here? Rapid disengagement loomed.

I said, "How many clients like Bill — if client is the right word for it — do the toads have?"

"We know of four," Fields said. "There may be others too embarrassed to admit they've been to the tub. We know of several who have respectfully declined. Or who have not so respectfully told Jim and Steven to go fuck themselves."

"This is highly unusual," I said. "It's really a weird way of getting recreational sex. If they have all this money and no one is eager to hop in the tub with the toads and their doggie, why don't they hire call boys? Men of their background and means have been known to take this approach. Does one of the toads have a background in finance or banking or something that makes them want to get off by injecting interest rates into the sexual equation? I have to say, this is novel."

"Jim was a corporation mouthpiece, and Steven's family had a couple of restaurants in Springfield, and apparently he did well on his own in banking," Fields said. "What they do with their hot-tub operation is less about money than it is about control. It's about making local gay men beholden to them, and about letting others know they can get away with it. It's more a power trip than a money trip, I think."

If what Fields was telling me about Sturdivant and Gaudios was true — sex in a hot tub in return for discounted interest rates — there still seemed to be an important element missing, psychologically or practically. There were too many simpler, easier ways to attain both sex and social preeminence for those who sought them. There had to be more to this.

I said, "Barry, I do understand why you're upset about being investigated just before your wedding to Bill. It must be annoying — and embarrassing. Do you have family around here who might get wind of my nosing around about you? Family members who might be planning to attend the wedding?"

Radziwill grew suddenly alert, but Fields just laughed. "Nice try, Don. What did the toads tell you about what I told them about my family?"

"It has not been established," I said, "that Sturdivant, Gaudios and I discussed you or anything about you. Perhaps I was dining with them this evening to analyze the musical pros and cons of the Tanglewood season. Levine is reported to be doing a bang-up job. I heard the Mahler was spectacular and the Mozart excellent, too. Or maybe our dinner at Pearly Gates wasn't musical at all, and I was meeting with the toads to negotiate a loan for myself."

Hazel-eyed Josh, still in his waiter's green and black get-up, jumped right in. "Hey, I heard you with the toads talking about Barry and about Tom Weed's death. And about asking around town about Barry. I wondered what it was you were talking about, but it was definitely about Barry, so don't try to deny it."

They all looked at me balefully.

"Josh," I said, "isn't there some high-end-restaurant protocol about customer confidentiality? You're quite the little Aunt Blabby."

"And you're quite the fucking 'stick your nose in other people's business' sleazy private eye asshole fucking jerk!" Fields spat out, suddenly flaring. His blue eyes blazed, and he seemed as if he might lunge at me but was working hard at controlling the impulse. Radziwill and Josh tensed and watched Fields and me somberly.

I said, "Barry, a few hours ago I knew much less about you and your situation and relationships than I know now. Had I known earlier everything you have just told me — providing that all of your story is true and that you're not withholding anything material — I might not have continued with my investigation. And what I'm thinking now is, I should just back off and get out of everybody's hair here in this pleasant town. Are you reassured by that?"

"No, I am *not* reassured. If you quit, those two will just hire some other cynical goon like yourself to start digging up my private life!" Fields' face was flushed, and he leaned toward me shaking and waving a clenched fist. "My life is my life, and only I will be in control of it! Who I am and what I am is nobody's damn business, and those two evil queens are not going to get away with this! It's time somebody put a stop to those two, and I'm going to do it! Jim and Steven are done, they are finished, they are *dead!* And you, Mister Albany Private Snooper, had just better fucking get out of the way, if you know what's good for you!"

Getting out of the way sounded like a good idea, though I guessed rightly that it wasn't going to be as simple as that.

CHAPTER FIVE

Having moved on to some routine background-checking for an Albany lawyer friend, I phoned Preston Morley in Stockbridge on Thursday morning, two days after my Great Barrington visit. I told him, "Thanks for sending the toads my way. You're a sweetheart, Preston. I plan on returning the favor some day, so I'd advise you to be on the lookout for skunks in your garbage can or the odd moose stepping on your car. When it happens, I want you to know I was the man behind it."

"Donald, my friend, what's this you say about skunks and moose and amphibians? Are we doing *Carnival of the Animals?* Or is it *The Wizard of Oz?* And instead of 'lions and tigers and bears!' it's 'skunks and moose and amphibians!' Clue me in, Donald, on the significance of these obscure literary or natural references, and then let's see where we might go from there."

Morley was the resident dramaturge and a frequent director of plays at the Stockbridge Theater Festival, and a Georgetown classmate of Timmy's. Two summers before, we had attended Morley's wedding to David Murano, a Pittsfield elementary school teacher, an event so thrillingly emancipating that Timmy and I had considered abandoning Albany and moving thirty miles eastward to the Gay Peoples Republic of Massachusetts. That way, we too could legitimize our foul-in-the-eyes-of-the-state union and flaunt our lifestyle in Antonin Scalia's front parlor, in the unlikely event that we should find ourselves down at Nino's house being served prune juice with rue. It was mainly Timmy's longtime financially rewarding and otherwise satisfying job with Assemblyman Lipshutz and both of our morbid attachments to the mauve charms of socio-political Albany that kept us where we were.

I said to Morley, "You don't know who I mean by *the toads?*"

"I do not. Is this an Old Testament reference, Donald? If so, I should be getting it, being a Georgetown alum. Although the New Testament did receive considerably more attention at that resplendently Jesuit institution, as I recall."

"Didn't you refer Jim Sturdivant and Steven Gaudios to me? They said you did."

"Oh, *those* toads."

"They hired me at your suggestion, Preston. That's what they said. Thanks ever so much."

"God, aren't they awful? I did run into Jim recently, and he asked if I knew of any private investigators, and before I could catch myself your name just popped out. You're not only the only private eye I know, you're the only one I've ever even heard of in this area. So maybe I was just showing off saying I knew a real-life gumshoe. I take it that your experience with Jim and Steven has not been fulfilling. If so, I do beg your forgiveness for my even mentioning your name. Go ahead. Have a moose step on my car."

I said, "I should have called you before I got mixed up with them. So it was my mistake. Anyway, it didn't work out. I did a little work for them, decided I did not wish to continue in their employ, and then phoned them yesterday morning and cut myself loose. So it's yet another lesson for me in checking out clients, especially before I check out anybody else for them."

"Timmy says you've had some doozies over the years."

"Most of my clients have been decent, ordinary people who have felt victimized or potentially victimized in ways where legal action was inappropriate or would have been personally awkward for one reason or another. But sometimes clients want to use investigators for their own dubious or even illegal ends. It's a hazard of the profession. When I get one of those — and when I manage to find out in time — I provide a refund and disengage. It's part ethical, part a matter of hanging on to my license."

"And were Jim and Steven crooks or just dubious types?"

"I can't really go into the details of what they wanted," I said. "Suffice is to say they misrepresented themselves and they misrepresented the facts, and yesterday I suggested they drop the matter they hired me to look into."

Morley said, "Could a Barry Fields have been involved? Something about protection from Barry Fields? I realize you may not be in a position to answer that question."

What was this? "Why do you ask?" I said.

"Because Barry Fields attacked Jim Sturdivant in a grocery store yesterday afternoon. It's in today's *Berkshire Eagle*. You don't know about this?"

"No. Unless it'd been a homicide or it involved a New York State elected official or his mistress or his underage boyfriend, it wouldn't make the Albany paper. What's the story?"

"It happened in Guido's, a fancy market in Great Barrington. Do you know it?"

"Of course. People from Albany drive over to Great Barrington just to shop there."

"So apparently Jim and Steven were in there yesterday around two doing their shopping when they ran into Barry Fields, a local gay guy who is about as fond of them as most people are, and they got into an argument about something. Anyway, Fields ended up screaming at the toads, and he hit Jim with a wheel of cheese."

"Was Sturdivant hurt?"

"Not badly, according to the paper. Not hospitalized, at any rate."

"Perhaps it was a fine, aromatic, soft cheese."

"The report didn't say. The *Eagle* is not what it once was, Donald. It's owned by a cheap chain now, and you're lucky if they don't spell cheese with a *z*. The old *Eagle* would have described the area in western France where the cheese originated and included a sidebar about the editor's mother's visit there in 1958."

"So was Barry Fields arrested?"

"The altercation was broken up by store employees and bystanders, but the police were called and Fields was hauled off. There was a hearing in Southern Berkshire District Court, and Fields was released on bond and ordered to stay away from the toads. The judge probably didn't state it exactly that way. Presumably he used their actual names."

"He must not have been acquainted with them."

"The other thing was — and this seems to me rather serious — Fields threatened to kill Sturdivant, according to some of the witnesses. Or at least to get rid of him. That's what the witnesses said Fields said. They said he said he was going to get rid of Jim once and for all, and that people would thank him for it. Now there's a remark that's not going to help him if he goes on trial for assault.

"So, Don," Morley asked, "what can you tell me? Do you know about what's going on here?"

"I think I do know, but I can't tell you, Preston. At least not until we see what's about to leak or spew out. Do you know Fields yourself?"

"Slightly. He lives with Bill Moore, a computer guy we once had in here to solve a box office crisis. Our computer was printing tickets with the number seven in front of every word on the ticket. Bill got rid of the sevens. We never knew what he did with them. I've heard Moore and Fields are getting married later this month. David and I know some people who are going to the wedding."

"Do you know either Fields' or Moore's families?"

"No. I don't think either of them is local."

"How about Bud Radziwill? He's a pal of Fields'."

"Oh, sure. The Kennedy cousin, so-called. So-called by Radziwill, but not by anybody else."

"That's the one."

"The thing is, there are some actual Kennedy cousins around here, and they laugh when anybody asks them about Radziwill. He claims to be related to Lee Radziwill, the Bouvier with the Polish aristocrat ex-husband. I know somebody who dated Bud for a while several years ago, and this guy said Radziwill did seem to speak with a slight Polish accent."

I said, "What have you heard about the toads' financial affairs? Anything about money-lending?"

"Do you mean like banking?"

"Like banking, but more informal."

"I wouldn't know about that. But the two do seem to be well off. Jim cleaned up, I'm sure, doing PR for defense and utilities companies, and Steven made money in investment banking, I believe. They always donate to the theater. That's basically how I know them."

"Have you ever been to their house?"

"Once, yes. They did a cocktail-party fundraiser before our annual gala. Nice place. Gorgeous big Victorian manse. Gardens, pool, hot tub. No tennis court, as I recall."

"Did you slide in, Preston?"

"Did I what?"

"Did you get in the hot tub with Jim and Steven?"

A pause. "You know, Donald, I'd forgotten those stories. If you're referring to what you seem to be referring to."

"I am."

"Well, most of the STF board was there when I was there, and twenty or thirty other theater donors. The hot tub was not being operated on that occasion. There were lovely hors d'oeuvres, I'm sure, but I expect that the snacking was limited to mushrooms with goat cheese in a light phyllo."

"Did you ever hear of Jim and Steven coercing men into their hot tub? In exchange for financial favors?"

Another pause. "Not for money, just for...oh. Oh crap."

"Oh crap what?"

"Oh crap."

"Yeah?"

"I know somebody who borrowed money from Jim once. A young actor who returns here every summer. I'd better not mention his name. You would recognize it."

"And?"

"Oh crap."

"Were there unconventional conditions attached to the loan agreement? Is that the oh-crap part that you just figured out?"

Morley said, "I assumed the upsetting conditions were financial when the borrower alluded to them. But he said something that afternoon about being exhausted from collecting his loan, and it struck me as odd at the time. Oh...yeeesh!"

"You bet."

"So...was Barry Fields another of the toads' banking customers? Do you think that's what the fight was about in Guido's yesterday?"

"I can't say any more about it just yet, Preston. But I appreciate your pretty much confirming someone else's story of similar bad behavior by those two. It's no surprise to me that someone would wallop one of them with a wheel of cheese. It's amazing they have avoided even worse, and it's good that the law is restraining Barry Fields from further contact."

"You know, Donald, I seem to recall David saying something about Jim having something shady in his past, but I can't remember what it was. Jim is originally from Pittsfield, and I think David's family might have had some distant connection to the Sturdivants. I'll ask him."

"Thanks, I'd be curious. Though I'm well out of Sturdivant's life now. I got out before he got hit with the groceries, so at this point it's mainly just gossip to me."

Mainly gossip but, I understood, not entirely gossip. It was I, after all, who had stuck my nose into Barry Fields' business, probably triggering his violent tantrum over the toads' meddling, which had included me as their perhaps too willing instrument.

I forgave Morley for mentioning me to Sturdivant. His intentions were good — sending business my way — and he had guessed rightly that I had suffered far worse clients over the course of my checkered career.

I went back to my phone and Internet digging. I spent half an hour gathering information on the deadbeat Hummer-dealer husband of an Albany nail-parlor operator who had hired a lawyer friend of mine to extract additional support for the couple's four children from the bad-citizen/bad-dad.

Then, around ten-fifteen, my cell phone rang, and it was Preston Morley again.

"Donald! Donald! Have you heard?"

"Heard what? I guess not."

"Someone in the office heard it on the radio. Jim Sturdivant was killed last night. Murdered!"

I asked myself two things. One, was I going to see the Berkshires again without having to wait for the next Tanglewood season? I guessed I would. The second question was, had I somehow done this?

CHAPTER SIX

"I'm Bill Moore. I need your help. You know who I am."

"Yes, I do know who you are."

The phone had rung not ten minutes after I had hung up with Preston Morley. In those ten minutes, I had found the *Berkshire Eagle*'s Web site, where a brief story had already been posted on the murder of James Sturdivant of Sheffield, a village south of Great Barrington. Sturdivant had been shot dead in his home at around nine o'clock the night before. His partner, Steven Gaudios, was not home at the time, but Sturdivant's wire-haired terrier had apparently tried to protect his master, and he also was gunned down. Police had a suspect in the shooting, the *Eagle* reported, and he was being sought for questioning.

Moore said, "The police think Barry shot Sturdivant. They think this because of the fight at Guido's yesterday. Are you aware of that incident?"

I said I was.

"But Barry did not shoot Sturdivant."

"Okay."

"Do you know why I'm calling you? Bud Radziwill suggested you were a decent human being who knew what you were doing. I double-checked. The reports I received were ambiguous about the know-what-you're doing part, and not everyone in Albany thinks of you as decent. But overall you come well recommended. So I'd like to hire you."

"To do what, Bill?"

"To clear Barry."

"Uh huh."

"Will you do it?"

"Won't the facts clear him? Doesn't he have an alibi?"

A pause. "Not exactly. Tuesdays and Wednesdays are Barry's nights off at the theater, where he would normally be working at the time the shooting is believed to have happened, around nine. Instead, he was alone at our house. I was working late on a job in Springfield. But Barry was home when I arrived just after eleven."

"Watching a movie on TMC?"

This reference to the circumstances surrounding Tom Weed's sad demise was probably unfair, and Moore swallowed hard. "Of course. That's what Barry does at night. He has ADD, and he's not much of a reader. And he loves old movies. He was watching television when I got home, and he had not left the house all evening."

"Did you ask him what movie he'd watched on TMC? Have the police asked him?"

Moore breathed hard. "Well, here's the thing. The thing is, Barry has disappeared. The police are looking for him."

"Where did he go?"

"I just said he disappeared."

"Yeah, I heard you, Bill. But you are the man Barry is planning to marry later this month. I'll bet you a dollar to a donut that he told his fiancé — that would be you — where he could be reached."

"Well, he didn't. And it's driving me crazy. I'm worried sick."

What a crock. "If that's your story."

"So will you help clear Barry?"

"Sure."

"You will?"

"Yes."

"Based on what I've heard about you, I thought you would. You might even say you owe it to Barry. In a very real sense, you precipitated — you and the toads, that is — you all precipitated the events that led to Barry being considered a suspect. I think you must know you bear at least partial responsibility for this entire goddamn mess."

"I can see where somebody might look at it that way. I guess I should be grateful Barry didn't shoot me."

"Barry didn't shoot anybody."

"He does have a temper, though. I've seen it."

"Yes, well, he comes by it honestly."

I was going to ask Moore what he meant by that, but he said the police were at his door and he had to go. We quickly made a plan to meet in Great Barrington at two, and then I phoned Timmy.

"I'm headed back to the Berkshires. Jim Sturdivant, one of the toads I told you about, has been shot dead. Barry Fields, one of the suspicious characters I was checking out for Sturdivant, is the chief suspect. He assaulted Sturdivant earlier in the day and threatened to get rid of him. Fields made similar threats in my presence Tuesday night. Now I've been hired by Fields' boyfriend to clear him of the murder."

"Oh, that's awful. Good luck, Donald. But how do you know Fields didn't do it?"

"I don't know that. But if I find out he did do it, I'll turn his ass over to the police and sue his boyfriend for my large fee in the event he should refuse to pay it."

"Well, that certainly sounds like truth, justice and the American way."

"I appreciate that I'm a little tetchy about all this. I'm not sure how much of it I set in motion by letting myself be used so shabbily by the toads."

"I wondered if you might be feeling that way. But as soon as you got the picture of what the toads were probably really doing, you backed off. You're clean, Don. Anyway, that must be why the boyfriend hired you. He sees you as potentially more friend than foe."

"Yes, or he sees me as an annoying troublemaker who might be turned into a useful troublemaker. I'm not sure what any of these people are up to. There remains the mystery of Fields' and Bud Radziwill's origins. Who were — or who are — these guys anyway? Plus, Fields has now disappeared."

"He ran away? That looks bad, no?"

"I'm sure the police have an opinion. The boyfriend, Bill Moore, claims not to know where Fields is. It's going to be hard to clear the guy unless I can find him. So I may be spending a lot of time in Great Barrington over the next days. Or elsewhere."

"Just don't you get shot, okay? Or arrested. I don't know about the cops over there, but I've heard the Berkshire County DA is a hard case, inflexible and mean. Don't get caught in his gun sights if you can avoid it. Metaphorically speaking, is what I think I mean."

"Timothy, I always think of the Berkshires as so benign. All those pretty fields and hills, and Verdi and James Taylor, and Mark Morris swooping around waving his love handles. I've always loved the place. I hope I don't come back from Massachusetts disillusioned."

"Yeah, or with your ass in a sling."

"Or my head on a platter."

"Or your nose out of joint."

"Or my testicles undescended."

"I'd help you find them."

"You always do."

Being on the phone with Timmy Callahan always cheered me up. But the good cheer didn't last, as was to be expected.

CHAPTER SEVEN

I arrived in Great Barrington an hour before my meeting with Bill Moore, so I drove on down to Sheffield to get a look at the crime scene. With the help of MapQuest — I ignored its routing through Bolivia — I found the Sturdivant–Gaudios house, a grand, white, maple-shaded Victorian, with neat lawns and tall stands of late-summer cosmos and phlox, and yellow crime-scene tape running from tree to tree around much of the property. Except for the police presence and the three TV news trucks parked out front, the place was so sweetly, anachronistically placid, I half expected Edith Wharton and Henry James to come strolling down the sidewalk together, James discoursing on the rosebushes at the house next door, Mrs. Wharton leading her two tiny Pekingese and smoking a doobie.

I parked across the street and got out just as a gaggle of reporters and camera crews emerged from behind the house and spread out quickly toward their cars and news vans. Crossing the street, I ducked under the police tape and walked up the driveway where the reporters had been. I could see the pool fenced off beyond the three-car garage and, I thought, the infamous hot tub. There were two Beemers, one convertible and one sedan, in the open garage, the American well-to-do doing their bit to help Bavaria.

I was about to turn back to the front of the house when the back door opened and Steven Gaudios came out followed by a uniformed state trooper. Gaudios recognized me and strode over looking gaunt and agitated.

"Well, Donald, you're a little late, aren't you, to be of any help to us whatsoever? A fat lot of good you did for us, protecting us from that lunatic! We *told* you he was dangerous, and you didn't believe us, and now look what has happened!"

I said, "Steven, I'm very sorry about Jim."

"Sorry? What is sorry? Sorry would be if you had protected Jim, the way you were supposed to, against that insane Barry Fields!"

"I wasn't hired to protect anybody, Steven. I was hired to check into Fields' background."

"Who are you?" the cop said, suddenly interested in me as more than an intruder.

I introduced myself, and he told me he was Trooper Joe Toomey, the detective assigned to the case. I gave him a quick rundown on my brief employment by Sturdivant and Gaudios. I said I had parted ways with the couple the day before on account of a disagreement over whether or not it was fair for them to be investigating Barry Fields. I thought, *Let's just get this out in the open now*, in the event Gaudios had neglected to mention it. For the moment, I did not bring up the toads' eccentric lending practices, though all of their clients might now be considered potential suspects in Sturdivant's murder.

"We should talk," the cop said and gave me his card. "What are you doing over here now?" He was fiftyish and clear-eyed, pint-sized and lean, and had a half-moon-shaped scar on one clean-shaven cheek.

I said, "I've been hired by Bill Moore, Barry Fields' fiancé, to help clear Fields. Moore feels certain Fields did not shoot anybody last night." I watched Toomey to see if he'd flinch when I used the term *fiancé* — he did not — and I watched Gaudios, knowing he would be outraged that I was now helping the man he thought had killed his ... spouse? No, for family reasons, Sturdivant had said, he and Gaudios had not married when so many long-term Massachusetts gay couples had.

On cue, and understandably, Gaudios began sputtering and intermittently weeping. "How can you do this! How can you *do* this! Barry even shot What-Not. You're a traitor, Donald. How can you do this to us! It's all just...unreal! I keep thinking it's all a nightmare and I'll wake up and it will all go away and Jim will be back in my life, where he belongs."

Gaudios went on for another minute, flushed and hysterical, while the cop and I stood helplessly. When Gaudios wound down, I said, "Steven, I know you believe Barry shot Jim, but there's no real evidence of that, is there?" I hoped

Detective Toomey might jump in here and add something — anything — to the little I knew, but he just watched me and said nothing.

Gaudios said, "Of course it was Barry. Barry attacked Jim in Guido's yesterday and threatened to kill him, and he was arrested. He was arrested, and the judge let him go! I hold that damn rotten judge responsible, too!"

"What was the argument in Guido's about?" I asked. "They were arguing and Barry hit Jim, but what set all that off?"

Gaudios started to speak, then waited. He was collecting his thoughts. He said, "It was about you, among other things."

"Oh?"

"Thanks to your ineptitude, Barry found out that Jim had asked you to investigate Barry. He was upset about that and blamed Jim." There was no mention of Fields' anger over the Bill Moore loan, which it appeared Gaudios had neglected to mention to the police.

The cop had been taking all this in with interest. He looked my way and said, "Mr. Gaudios tells me that Barry Fields has an unknown past. That you checked him out and learned that he has no verifiable existence earlier than six years ago. We're doing our own checking, but is that what you came up with, Mr. Strachey?"

"It is."

"And now Fields seems to have vanished into the Neverland he came out of."

"He's gone, I'm told, yes. But he could have run off because he's your prime suspect following yesterday's altercation in the grocery store, and he has no alibi for last night. He's innocent, but he panicked and fled. This happens."

"It does," Toomey said, "but guilty people run away too. That happens even more often. I suppose you'll be trying to locate Fields, like me. If you find him, it is your obligation to bring him in or to notify me or other investigating officers as to his whereabouts. Are you clear about that?"

"I know the law," I said. "My intention here is to do what's right."

"We'll appreciate any help you can give us," Toomey said. "Just don't fuck with me."

"You bet."

"Or the DA. Are you familiar with the Berkshire County district attorney, Thorne Cornwallis?"

"No, I'm not."

"People call him Thorny for a reason. So I look forward to any assistance you can render, and your cooperation with the district attorney's office is something I know we can all count on."

What was this, Chitlin Switch, Georgia? This was not the Berkshires I knew. Where were all the pretty James Taylor tunes?

I said, "If Fields is innocent, I'll convince you of that, detective. If he's guilty, he's all yours. And Thorny's."

Gaudios said, "Thorne Cornwallis is an excellent crime-fighter. Jim and I have supported him for years. I am completely confident that he'll put Barry Fields away in Walpole for the rest of his life, and I'm only sorry that Massachusetts no longer executes cold-blooded killers like Barry."

"Steven," I said, "I want to see justice done here as much as anybody. So, please tell me. What happened last night?" I thought Toomey might cut this off, but he was smart enough to see the advantage of having Gaudios go through his story one more time.

"Oh, it was so awful, Donald! So, so awful!"

"You were out for the evening?"

"I played bridge with Nell Craigy and two of her regulars. Trill Gallagher was ill, and they needed a fourth, and I volunteered. We had a few martinis —" Gaudios noted Toomey's presence and corrected himself "— we had a few martinis but no more than two, and so I didn't get out of there until ten forty-five. When I arrived home around eleven, I expected to find Jim in bed watching TV, but..." Gaudios began to choke up again. We waited for a long moment while he struggled and then regained control. He went on, "But I knew something was wrong when What-Not didn't race to the back door when I came in and jump into my arms. The house was so...so *still*. And then I walked through the dining room and into the foyer, and...and...I *saw* them." He shook his head and cried. Both Toomey and I lowered our gaze, though not so low that we weren't keeping a peripheral eye on Gaudios as he recalled the grisly scene and reacted.

While Gaudios wept, Toomey picked up the narrative. "Jim Sturdivant had been shot three times, twice in the chest, once in the back of the head," the cop said. So the shooter clearly wanted Sturdivant dead. "The dog apparently came to Mr. Sturdivant's defense, and he was shot twice and killed. Sturdivant was facing his assailant when he was shot in the chest, and he fell backwards near the front door of the house. Apparently he had let the killer into the house, suggesting that the shooter was someone he knew."

This got Gaudios back in action. "Barry! It just had to have been Barry!"

I said, "And no other shots were fired?"

"Just the five nine-millimeters," Toomey said.

"Did anyone hear the gunfire?" I said. "There are all these houses nearby."

"Several people did hear the shots," Toomey said, "and phoned the county emergency dispatcher just after nine. Officers in a patrol car from the Lee barracks arrived at nine forty but, finding the neighborhood calm, left the scene. The neighbors have been interviewed, and none of them saw anybody arrive at or depart the Sturdivant home at the time of the gunfire. The shooter may have parked a block away and cut through back yards."

"I suppose your forensics guys have checked the yards," I said.

"Yeah, you can suppose that."

"Did I see a swimming pool out back there? And a hot tub?"

Gaudios said, "Anybody going through the yard would see the pool. We've got floodlights with motion sensors back there. And the pool is fenced in. We'll be...we would have been.... I'll have to close the pool soon. We start getting leaves this time of year." He got teary again, and I thought about what my life would be like without Timothy Callahan, and then I pushed that thought out of my head.

I said, "The circumstances of this shooting don't look to me like anger or pique — the kind of mayhem you'd expect if an amateur like Barry Fields went bonkers after a fight in a grocery store. This looks like an assassination. Professional almost. The killer walked in, shot Sturdivant and the dog, and walked out again.

"How do you know Fields is an amateur?" Toomey said.

I had no answer to that. For all any of us knew, six years earlier Fields could have worked for a Columbian drug cartel or the Pakistani intelligence services. I said, "Does anyone know if Fields owned a gun?"

"He never registered one. But in your line of work you must know about the ready availability of illegal firearms, Mr. Strachey. It's like shopping for a leaf blower. Maybe easier. Certainly cheaper."

"I do know."

"No, Barry Fields is definitely our prime suspect. He attacked Jim Sturdivant earlier in the day yesterday, and he threatened to get rid of him, according to witnesses. And his flight pretty much nails it, to my way of thinking. I appreciate your wanting to earn your fee from Bill Moore. But you're pushing against the obvious here."

"What about Sturdivant's business and personal life? Isn't there anybody else who might have had it in for him?"

This got Gaudios's prompt attention, but he said nothing.

Toomey said, "Mr. Sturdivant has been retired from the business world for four years. According to Mr. Gaudios, he didn't have an enemy in the world and has pretty much devoted his life to performing good deeds for friends and charities."

"But," I said, "you must have spoken to Bill Moore. I know for a fact that his opinion of Jim Sturdivant was more critical. Maybe there were others who also thought ill of Jim."

Gaudios's face tightened, and Toomey gave me a bemused look that told me something I needed to know. *So*, I thought, *Toomey knows about the loans and probably about the conditions. And Gaudios knows Toomey knows, and now they both know that I know that they both know.*

"Don't you worry, Mr. Strachey, that we'll miss one single important angle," Toomey said. "This crime was committed just last night, and my investigation has just begun. And now that we've met and I see what a solid professional you are, I'm going to want to count on you to share your skills and judgment and professionalism with those of us employed to solve this crime for the people of Massachusetts. Can I count on you?"

"You sure can, detective. I'm at your service. Yours and Thorny's."

Expressionless, Toomey studied me closely, and Steven Gaudios stood looking bereft and apprehensive.

CHAPTER EIGHT

Bill Moore's house was set up on a hillside on the east side of Great Barrington, separated from the business district by the Housatonic River. The Housatonic's pretty but modest flow would be labeled a creek or brook in New York State and most others, but in New England every topographical dribble was called a river, part of the region's quirky old-country charm. Moore's white, wood-frame two-story house was identical to millions of others in the woodier regions of North America, and it was barely visible behind a profusion of bushes and trees. It seemed to be the abode of someone who preferred privacy or even anonymity, or maybe he just found it pleasant.

I parked in the driveway behind a beige Honda, climbed up six or eight steps, and rang the doorbell. There were some old green wicker chairs on the porch, but they looked dusty and unused. The door swung open.

"Donald Strachey?"

"Yep. Bill Moore?"

"Come on in."

I saw why Fields had gone for a man twenty years older than he was. Moore was impressive to behold, with a middleweight college wrestler's build and a green-eyed George Bellows-painting athlete's mug. He had close-cropped light hair with some gray in it and rings of sleeplessness around his watchful eyes. Barefoot in old khakis and a faded red T-shirt, Moore carried just enough of an incipient paunch to suggest that although he liked to keep fit, he was not fetishistic about it.

"Have a seat," Moore said. "Did you eat?"

"Had a sandwich in the car. Thanks."

The living room looked disconcertingly like a straight guy's bachelor pad, with a lot of nondescript black leather seating, most of it facing a TV set the size of a stadium scoreboard. The floor was not littered with Budweiser dead soldiers, but there was an empty pizza box on the coffee table. The only sign that homosexuals as we generally think of them might have lived here was a bookshelf against one wall that was stuffed with movie and movie-lore titles. There were screenplays, biographies of stars and directors, picture books, plus history and criticism, including what looked like the complete Pauline Kael. I guessed these belonged to Barry Fields, and wherever he had fled to — Colorado? Waziristan? upstairs? — he had not taken his movie books with him.

I said, "I was just down in Sheffield and met Detective Toomey at the crime scene."

"Good. You're getting right to work. I'm reassured already."

"Toomey seems single-minded but not bull-headed. He's after Barry, but if we can show that Barry could not have shot Sturdivant, Toomey is smart enough to grasp it. Don't you think?"

Sitting across from me, Moore sighed and shook his head. "I don't know about Toomey. He might be okay. It's Thorne Cornwallis, the DA, I'm worried about. He's unimpressed by facts if they look like they'll get in the way of a slam-dunk prosecution. Anyway, proving that Barry did not do the shooting will be tough. He has no alibi, and he *could* have done it. Except he didn't. For one thing, Barry has no gun. Barry hates guns."

"Do you own a firearm, Bill?"

He looked at me and shrugged. "I do. Detective Toomey asked me that too. It's a Glock-nine. It could have been the murder weapon. I keep it in the bedroom closet. When Toomey was here, I produced the weapon, and he took it in for analysis. It'll come back clean, so we don't have to worry about that."

I said, "How come you own a gun? Great Barrington doesn't feel much like Dodge."

"I lived in DC for eleven years. It's a dangerous place. A woman was shot in the lobby of my building. Killed for the eight dollars in her handbag."

"Where was that?"

"Where I lived?"

"Yeah. I know DC a little. I like it. I like its cosmopolitan-ness. Even though it's a cosmopolitan city that's basically run by people from Kansas."

Moore seemed momentarily startled when I said this, though at the time I had no idea why.

He said, "I lived in the Dupont Circle area, New Hampshire near Eighteenth. Very gay, even though I was not very out at the time. That took a while longer." Remembering this, Moore looked sad.

"You retired from the federal government early, I was told."

"Five years ago, yeah."

"Which agency?"

"That's another life."

"I think Jim Sturdivant said you worked for the Commerce Department."

"Yeah, well."

"Did you and Barry meet in DC?"

"No, we met after I moved up here."

"Uh huh."

Moore sat looking at me, and then he seemed to realize he was talking like an anxious man with something to hide. He perked up a little and said, "I was attracted to Barry, but I thought he was Tom Weed's boyfriend. Do you know about Tom?"

I nodded.

"So it wasn't until Tom died that I made my move. And it turned out that Barry was attracted to me all along, but he had thought I wasn't interested. We wasted a lot of time, but we finally got it right. We got it very right, in fact. I was never so happy or sure of anything in my whole life. And then you came along." He looked at me, waiting for me to justify or explain my despicable interference.

I said, "Yes, Bill, I was hired by Sturdivant to check Barry out — because, Sturdivant told me, he was concerned that Barry was going to rip you off in some way. It sounded like a plausible enough story at the time."

Moore leaned back and snorted. "What shit."

"Apparently."

"Barry told me Sturdivant told you I was his good buddy. But Barry told you the truth — what my real relationship was with Jim."

"He did."

"I only knew Sturdivant socially and didn't particularly like him or Gaudios. But I borrowed forty thousand dollars from Jim at a better rate than I could have gotten at any bank. He offered this to me, 'as a friend,' he said at the time. The exact nature of the 'friendship' didn't become apparent until the day I went over to pick up the check — after I'd already signed the purchase agreement on this house." Moore shook his head dolefully.

"And then it was into the hot tub, with Jim and Steven?"

"It was never spelled out," Moore said. "But when Jim said he'd give me the check after we relaxed a bit in the tub, and why didn't I get naked, I knew immediately what was going on. My first impulse was to laugh, and my second impulse was to tell the toads to go fuck themselves. And then I thought, hell, what a quick and easy and totally uncomplicated way to knock half a point in interest off a major loan."

I said, "What with Alan Greenspan not being available to do his bit."

"So I asked, will I have to do this more than once? And Jim said, no, not unless you have such a wonderful time you want to come back for more. So — what the hell."

"And you climbed in, and then you just closed your eyes and thought of...not England. Where are you from originally, Bill?"

"The Midwest. So anyway, I saved myself a few thousand dollars that day. And, I can tell you, it wasn't the most humiliating thing I've ever done sexually."

"We all have our stories."

"And then, of course, I found out later that I wasn't the only borrower with an unwritten hot tub clause in my contract. There are four other guys, and I'll bet more."

"May I have their names? They could be considered possible suspects in the murder. You don't seem especially angry about the loan conditions, just mildly disgusted. But some people might get rattled by treatment like this, or even unhinged. Then there's the question of repayment of the loan. I take it you're not off the hook, and neither are the other borrowers. Or are you?"

"I assume I now owe thirty-four thousand three hundred dollars to Jim's estate. I certainly don't plan to welch on the loan. I don't know about the other guys. You'd have to ask them."

I said, "What was Barry's reaction to the hot-tub incident?"

"He was grossed out, naturally. But this was before we were together. I told him later."

"Detective Toomey didn't say anything, but I got the impression he knows about Sturdivant's lending practices. Was it you who filled him in?"

"You bet I did. I wanted him to know what kind of human being Jim Sturdivant was. I said if Sturdivant would pull crap like that, then he might be into all kinds of shit, and why were the cops just looking at Barry and not at anybody else?"

"What was Toomey's reaction?"

"He didn't seem all that interested. He never even asked me for the names of the other borrowers. I think I did get the point across that Sturdivant was a scumbag. But I got the impression that Toomey expected gay people to do all kinds of weird sexual stuff, and this was just par for the course, and he didn't really want to look into it or even think about it. A lot of people in law enforcement are like that. You must have noticed this, being in your line of work."

"I have, though in my experience there are fewer homophobes in the criminal justice system than there used to be. Albany has a long history of bigoted cops, and yet today the police chief is a PFLAG dad. Have you ever worked in law enforcement, Bill?"

"Why would you ask that?"

"You know guns. You slide right into cop terminology."

Moore laughed. "These days everybody uses cop language. It's all those CSI shows. I think it's funny."

"So you used to be in the police?"

"Not exactly. But I don't wish to talk about my past. With you or with anyone else." His face flushed, and he looked at me hard.

"How come?"

"It's not nice. We'll have to let it go at that."

I said, "Is Barry's past not nice too? Barry did not officially exist prior to six years ago."

"You'd have to ask Barry about that."

"Surely you know Barry's life story. You're planning on marrying the guy."

"It's not for me to tell. But this I can say. I'm telling you, Strachey, that Barry's past is totally irrelevant to the Sturdivant situation."

"And Bud Radziwill, so-called. He only came into existence when Barry did. What's that about? You guys are three awfully mysterious fellows. Am I being yanked around here in some unfortunate way? I'm starting to have a nauseating feeling about all of this and about all of you."

Moore thought hard about something for a long moment, and if he was getting the impression he might be losing me, that was fine. Because he was. Then he said, "I understand your frustration, Strachey. In fact, I've been there. Look, here's the thing. I'm going to confide in you. This goes no farther than this room, right? Are you capable of discretion? I think you are. You must be bound by *some* kind of professional ethics."

"Some kind, yes. But just spit it out, and then I'll tell you which ethics might apply. It's yours I'm worried about."

"The thing is, I was FBI. Twenty-one years. Ten in the field, eleven at the bureau."

"I see."

"I prefer to keep this quiet."

"Why?"

"People expect you to think and behave in a certain way. I don't want that. I'm out of that."

I said, "I know Great Barrington is some kind of hotbed of anti-Bush sentiment. There's an equestrian statue of Dennis Kucinich as you ride into town. But you were a professional. Most people respect that, even if they don't like the politically appointed doofuses, no? Or is that not what you mean?"

Moore slumped back in his chair, raised his muscular arms, and put his big hands behind his head. He squeezed his eyes shut. He said, "I made some mistakes. I don't want to go into it."

"That's up to you."

"It's just...hard."

"Were you fired?"

"No. I resigned. Retired."

"So it's nothing criminal."

He seemed to ponder this and said nothing.

I asked, "Does Toomey know about this?"

"No. It's not relevant."

"Does Barry know?"

"Sure. It's one of the things we have in common. We're different in a lot of ways. I'm older. I like computers and sports. Barry likes movies. But we both like the Berkshires, and the big thing is, we can understand each other because we both have pasts we want to forget."

"Can you tell me what Barry's past is that he wants to leave behind?"

Moore looked at me now and said, "Sorry, no. I swore I'd never tell a soul. Barry would be very, very upset."

"He does have a temper. You told me on the phone that Barry came by his hot temper honestly. What did you mean by that?"

Moore seemed to consider his reply, and said, "Just that he comes from a long line of hotheads."

"Uh huh. And what set off the confrontation in Guido's market yesterday?"

"Don't act surprised when I tell you it was *you* and your investigation you were doing for the toads — for Jim and Steven. Barry told me about his confrontation with *you* on Tuesday night after your dinner at Pearly Gates. Barry vented, and we smoked a joint, and he seemed to get over it. But then on Wednesday he ran into Jim and Steven in Guido's, and he got mad all over again. Jim got Barry going with some bullshit about protecting his loan, and then he *really* set Barry off by saying that he was looking out for my interests by protecting me from Barry. Unfortunately, a big piece of cheese was within reach, and Barry threw it at Jim. It's not a serious weapon, but under the law, assault is assault."

I said, "Has Barry hit people before?"

Moore thought this over. "I don't think so. He's really not a violent person, despite his anger. His occasional rage tends to come out verbally."

"What is Barry angry about?" I asked.

Moore said, "If I could tell you that — which I can't — you'd never believe it. Not in a million years."

CHAPTER NINE

I parked downtown off Main Street and made some calls from the car. I set up meetings with two of the four hot-tub borrowers — two others I was unable to reach — and with Bud Radziwill. I also arranged to meet Fields' boss at the movie theater, Myra Greene, a woman Moore said Fields was close to. I needed to (a) track down Fields and get his complete story — it seemed too far-fetched that the Sturdivant shooting was totally unrelated to Fields' altercation with him on the same day — and (b) get a clearer picture of the toads' lives and anybody else who might have wanted Jim dead. The circumstances of Sturdivant's death suggested not rage but calculation, and I needed to find out why that was so.

Moore had been meticulously unhelpful in speculating on where Fields had run off to. He said Fields had had no contact with his own family in years, and Moore stated implausibly that he didn't even know where they lived. He said all of Fields' current friends were in the Berkshires and each had told him that they had no idea where Fields went after he left in his car early that morning. Someone with a police scanner had tipped Fields off that Sturdivant had been shot, Moore said — he claimed not to know who — and Fields had sped off in his car at one in the morning, declaring that he would not return until the real killer had been caught. He had fled just in time, for the police came looking for him just twenty minutes later.

Moore had given me Fields' cell number, and I called it and got no answer. I left a message saying I wanted his help in finding the real killer and to please call me, and I was on his side.

None of Moore's story quite added up — his knowledge and understanding of Fields' behavior was far too selective — and on impulse I phoned an acquaintance at FBI headquarters in DC. I asked about the circumstances of William Moore's retirement from the bureau five years earlier. My contact, a former Albany cop drawn southward by the cachet and the eventual good pension benefits of federal employment, called me back in ten minutes with this information: four men named William Moore had been agents at the bureau during the past thirty years. Two were long since deceased; one was currently a twenty-seven-year-old special agent assigned to the San Diego field office; and the other William Moore was a man in his mid-sixties working as a ballistics expert at Washington headquarters. My contact said he had seen this Bill Moore in the lobby of the FBI building just a few days earlier. There was no William or Bill Moore in his late forties who had retired from the bureau five years earlier.

I thought, *Swell.* I had a retainer check in my pocket from Moore, and I decided I needed to get it back to Albany and into my bank fast.

I walked across Main Street under a gauzy late summer sky. Only a few of the leaves had begun to turn, and it felt more like August than September — except for the absence of the tourist-season throngs, many of them New Yorkers, the visitors and second-homers for whom downtown Great Barrington functioned as a kind of Columbus Avenue North. Though on this post-Labor Day lazy Thursday afternoon, the town felt more like a Truman-era burg, with maybe a car gliding by with its windows open and its radio tuned to a World Series with the Yanks and the Cards.

The Triplex Cinema, down a business-block passageway and out back beyond a parking lot, was plenty up-to-date. It looked like it had been smartly refashioned in recent years out of a warehouse or other non-artistic space. It was playing one pop hit of a not entirely repellent nature and two art-house features. A few customers had ambled in for the matinee showings, and I waited while Myra Greene sold them their tickets and gave the robot projectionists their orders.

As she led me up the stairs to her office in a loft over the concession stand, the tiny theater manager creaked and wheezed and showed the effects of what Bill Moore had told me were her eighty-nine years. Greene was bent and unsteady in her blue work pants and faded gray sweater, but peering out from her ruined face were alert black eyes, and when I introduced myself, her smile was a cracked version of Rita

Hayworth's. The distinct odor of nicotine and tar that trailed behind Greene was not abhorrent on her, the way it usually was in our fresh new largely tobacco-free world; on Greene it was pleasantly anachronistic, as if she were a grainy old newsreel from a more innocent time.

She saw me eyeing the Save-the-Thalia poster on the wall behind her desk, and as I took a seat across from her, Greene croaked out, "You old enough to remember the Thalia? I ran it for eleven years, ya know."

I did recall the long-gone famous repertory art house on Manhattan's Upper West Side, and I said I was impressed.

"Nowadays you can watch *Shoeshine* or *Nights of Cabiria* at home, so who gives a damn about the communal experience. Television didn't just kill the movies; it killed sitting in a dark theater with five hundred other people and keeping your mouth shut and feeling your common humanity." Greene tried to gesture with her head at the poster behind her, but she seemed to have trouble moving her neck.

I said, "This place seems to be carrying on at least part of the tradition nicely."

"It's good in the summer, and we make it through the winter. And we're appreciated. I'd like to screen some of the classics, though. We tried it, but too few people showed up. What does anybody need us for, when they can get *Rules of the Game* from Netflix?"

"I understand that Barry Fields is a real movie nut like yourself."

Greene squinted at me and said, "So you're a real-life private eye?"

"I am. Licensed by the state of New York."

"You're no Dick Powell and no Bogie either. And not at all Elliott Gould — though in a lot of ways he was my favorite Marlowe. Altman's *The Long Goodbye* is a wonderful picture, funny and textured, about awful old LA and the thug-ridden movie business. Pauline Kael, who loved it, said it finished off the hard-boiled genre. But luckily people like Frears and Curtis Hanson don't seem to have noticed."

I said, "I wish I had more time to delve into my fictional antecedents. But it's hard to do that when you're mainly trying to earn a living. Myra, I'm told you're going to retire next year, and that Barry Fields is going to take your place."

"So, Donald, give it to me straight. Are you packing heat?" She let loose with a phlegmy laugh, but this too seemed to hurt her neck and so she just grinned.

"I am not carrying a gat, Myra. I rarely do. Are you disappointed?"

"Let down, but not surprised. Anyway, you wouldn't want to get into a shootout around here. The Barrington cops were trained by the Ottoman Turks, and you wouldn't last long." Another hoarse chuckle.

"I've only met a statie so far," I said. "Trooper Joe Toomey. He's in charge of the Jim Sturdivant homicide. Did you know Sturdivant?"

Greene got a sour look. "I'm sorry Jim was killed. But, in truth, he was a pisher. The man charmed or intimidated or bought the people he needed. He ignored or walked over everybody else. I won't miss him, and you won't find many who will."

"The police think Barry Fields shot him. What do you think?"

"Not a chance," Greene said, stiffening and trying to throw her head back, except her neck wouldn't let her. "Barry hasn't got a violent bone in his body. He's tetchy and he can blow off. But that kid would never physically hurt a soul. It's asinine!"

"He did hit Sturdivant with a wheel of cheese yesterday."

She chortled again. "I saw that in the *Eagle.*"

"And maybe one thing led to another?"

"Don't bet on it."

"You read about the fight in the grocery store in the paper. Didn't Barry tell you about it himself?"

"He didn't mention it to me," Greene said and lowered her eyes from my gaze, as if she was embarrassed over telling this fib. "Barry just called me last night and said he needed to take some time off, and sorry about the short notice. I was lucky I was able to get somebody to cover for him tonight, this kid Annette who works for us part-time."

"What time did Barry call? As I mentioned on the phone, I'm trying to track him down. It's important for his defense that I get to him before the police do."

"It was late," Greene said. "I stay up all hours. I get by with four hours of sleep a night. I'll get plenty of rest any year now when it's time for me to sleep the you-know-what."

"*The Big Sleep?*"

She said, "Donald, very good."

"And do you own a police scanner, Myra? I'm just curious."

"No, Donald, as a matter of fact, I don't own one of those obnoxious squawk boxes. Why would I want to know what the real cops are doing, when I can pop *The Naked City* into my DVD player? Or Kubrick's *The Killing?*"

"But perhaps, Myra. you have a friend with a scanner?"

She looked down again and, I think, blushed. She was a fundamentally honest woman. And a good-hearted, well-intentioned co-conspirator for Fields, just not a very effective one.

"I won't ask you any more about that, Myra. But you really must try to understand what I'm saying. I can help Barry best if I know where he is and can speak to him personally. So where do you think Barry might have gone?"

She sighed and made her neck do something and said, "Beats me, kiddo. I wish I could help you out, but I can't. You...*you* have to understand."

"Bill Moore told me you're one of Barry's best friends in the Berkshires. A true friend in your situation would put Barry in touch with his most ardent advocate and protector. And that's the job I've been hired to do."

"It's a fact," she said, "that Barry and I are pals. I'm retiring next year — not because I want to or have to but because the SOBs who own this place are heaving me out the side door when I hit ninety. I don't know what they expect me to do. Dr. Greene, the dentist, who was twenty-six years older than I was, died while enjoying a full plate of rice, beans and *ropa vieja* in 1974. So what the hell am I supposed to do next? I'm married to this movie theater, and it's what keeps me going. Otherwise, what's the point? But Barry's in line for my job, and he's a good kid, and I hope he'll at least allow me to clean the johns, ya know?"

Greene's story was sad and all too familiar, but I wasn't sure whether she was telling it because it was what was on her mind or to stay off the subject of Barry Fields as long as she could get away with it. I guessed both.

I said, "Where do you live, Myra? Is Barry hiding out in your home?"

She rose an inch off her seat and fell back again. "Well, you've got balls of brass!"

"Yeah, and you know what? I think you do, too."

She gave me a faint smile now. "So, Donald. Does this mean you're going to send me over? I'm going to have to take the fall? Is it twenty to life in San Quentin for Myra?"

I said, "That's right, Myra. I'm not going to play the sap for you and I'm sending you over. But you're an angel. I'll wait for you. And if they hang you I'll always remember you."

Greene grinned. "Sam Spade and Brigid O'Shaughnessy. Bogart and Mary Astor. The movie words are right from the book," she said. "Huston told his secretary to type up the Hammett dialogue, and he pretty much wrote the screenplay from that transcript."

I looked at her and asked it again. "So, Myra, is Fields hiding in your house?"

"Nah."

"He couldn't have gone far. The police are looking for his car."

"*Ce n'est pas mon affaire.*"

"Do you live here in town?"

"I live in a lean-to out behind the theater. It's handy, ya see?"

"Like William Powell in *My Man Godfrey.*"

"Or the squatters in *Tsotsi.* But I do it by choice."

She wasn't going to budge, so I would have to learn elsewhere where Greene lived and then check the place out — not that the police wouldn't have been there first.

I said, "Myra, what do you know about Barry's personal history? Where's he from, anyway? I haven't been able to pick up much background on him."

"Oh," she said, "Barry never talked much about his life before he came to the Berkshires. Barry is not someone to be a slave to the past. He's a kid who's always looking ahead."

"But you're his friend. Aren't you curious?"

"Oh, sure, curious! But I'm a respecter of anybody's privacy. And Barry never wanted to talk about certain things."

She was being so evasive that I could only conclude that Greene was in on the big secret, too. She knew it. Moore knew it. Probably Bud Radziwill, since he may have shared the secret. And they all claimed — or likely would claim — that Fields' secret had nothing to do with Jim Sturdivant's murder. I was getting nowhere.

I said, "What do you know about Bud Radziwill?"

"Why do you ask? He's Barry's chum."

"He has an unknown past. Maybe he's an escaped criminal. That kid with a Texas twang can't possibly be named Radziwill. What does anybody really know about this guy?"

With a straight face, Greene said, "Bud is a Kennedy cousin. He spends holidays at the compound at Hyannis Port."

"Which holidays? Battle of the Alamo Day? Laura Bush's birthday? Come on."

She looked at me out of those dark eyes and tried to make a little shrug, but her neck misbehaved again and she grimaced.

"And Bill Moore," I said. "What do you know about Bill? Your friend Barry's going to marry the guy, after all."

"Isn't it wonderful?" Greene said. "Who'd've thought I'd live to see the day when gays could marry in the United States. I can remember when most people didn't even know what gay was. I had a cousin, Gabe Yellin, who lived for sixty years with a man named Amos, a plumber from New Rochelle, and people called them confirmed bachelors."

"Yes, but what about Moore? Is he a good match for Barry? Barry's so much younger, for one thing."

Greene grew somber. "It's not the age difference. I was twenty-six years younger than Dr. Greene, and I had no complaints and neither did he."

"Uh huh."

She said, "Isn't Bill your employer in this? You said he hired you to get Barry off the hook."

"True. I'm just trying to get a picture of Barry's life. It will be easier to convince others that he could not have killed Jim Sturdivant once I have convinced myself of this and fully understand the reasons for which I have come to believe absolutely in Barry's innocence. Myra, Bill Moore is Barry's fiancé, and you seem to have some reservations about him."

Her face crinkled up, and she looked her age more than ever. She said, "I don't know about Bill. I suppose he's fine if Barry says he is. But...I don't know."

"Why not?"

She hesitated, and said, "Maybe Bill killed somebody once. More than one person."

What was this? "What makes you think so?"

She looked over my shoulder, puzzling it out. "Bill always seemed depressive to me."

"Depressive?"

"He gets this haunted look. Especially after he's had a few beers.

I waited.

"He was drinking over at Twenty Railroad with Hal Stackmeyer one night, and he told Hal he had killed people and it was eating him alive. That's how he phrased it, Hal told me, 'eating him alive.' Hal was so shocked, he didn't ask any questions. And Bill didn't say any more. Just that he knew what it was like to take human lives and he didn't like the feeling. So I think Bill is not a happy person and maybe he can't ever be a truly happy person. And I sometimes wonder if Barry isn't making a mistake by hooking up with this depressed man. And Bill is even more depressed when he drinks. Which maybe he does too often. That's never a good sign."

I said, "Moore didn't give any indication of the circumstances of these murders?"

"Hal said no."

"Not whether or not it was work-related — military or law enforcement?"

"No."

"Myra, have you ever heard that Bill worked in law enforcement before he came to the Berkshires?"

"He's a computer guy. I thought that's what he did for the government." Then she thought about it and said, "Maybe CIA or something, and had to assassinate people. In Afghanistan or somewhere."

"Maybe," I said. "Though the timing isn't quite right for that. Unless it was pre-nine-eleven."

"Or maybe he killed people...like a criminal and he's wanted. Or he served time in prison and now he's out."

"Possibly."

"Or maybe he was drunk and he just made the whole thing up."

"Any of the above," I said.

CHAPTER TEN

The police found Barry Fields not in Myra Greene's house — which, being competent, they had had under surveillance since the night before — but in a summer house on nearby Lake Buel that was owned by a friend of Greene's and for which she had a key. A neighbor had spotted Fields moving his car into the garage just after dawn — as a Triplex employee, he had a familiar face around town — and when word got out that Fields was wanted in a murder investigation, the neighbor did his duty and called the cops. Fields was taken to the Great Barrington police lockup, pending a bail hearing at his arraignment the next morning.

I learned all this from Bill Moore, who called my cell phone just as I was leaving the Triplex and heading for Bud Radziwill's apartment, where I was to meet the famed Kennedy cousin.

"Barry was right here in town all along," Moore said.

To which I replied, "How astonishing."

"What do you mean?"

"You aren't straight with me about much of anything, Bill. Neither is anybody else I talk to in this town. Is Great Barrington the liars' capital of the Northeast, or what's the damn deal, anyway?"

"I'm not sure what you're referring to, Strachey."

"Of course you don't know which lie I'm referring to. There are so many of them. For one, you never worked for the FBI, Bill. I checked."

I could hear him breathing. Then he said, "You're good."

"Uh huh."

"But why is any of that relevant?"

"I don't know that it is relevant, Bill. Nor do I know that it isn't. How am I supposed to know the difference when everybody involved in this miasma is wearing a mask, and it seems as if just about everybody in town knows who is actually behind that mask except me. This leaves me at a distinct disadvantage. And it annoys the crap out of me, too."

"I hear where you're coming from, Strachey."

"Yeah, and...?"

"We'll have to talk."

"When?"

"Tomorrow — say, lunch? But meanwhile, Barry's being arraigned at nine in the morning in Southern Berkshire District Court. Can you be there?"

"I can. But let's us get together sooner. I need clarity — clarity and honesty and the truth about all of you — if I am to be at all helpful to you and to Barry. Do you get what I'm saying? Can I make it any clearer?"

"I have to work tonight. I'm behind on an installation job I should have finished today, and I'll be at the Lenox High School until late tonight. But I'll see you at the arraignment, and then we'll have lunch, and I'll fill you in on a few things. These are things that won't be helpful in clearing Barry. But if telling you these things relieves your mind, then it'll be worth it. Deal?"

Now what game was he playing? "Sure."

Moore said, "I just talked to Ramona Furst, Barry's lawyer on the assault charge, and she's agreed to represent him on the murder charge too. She's sure she can get Barry out, though the bail could be high. Ramona's good. You'll need to talk to her. She knows about you and is pleased that you're on the team."

I said, "Oh, there's a team? So far, everybody in this town I've met seems to be a rugged individualist. It's hot-dogger heaven here. I'm awfully glad that's about to change."

Moore said he had to get to the high school and would see me in the morning, and then he was gone.

I thought about dropping in on Myra Greene again to see what more I could pry out of her, now that she had been revealed as a dissembler and possible felon. But I had appointments with Radziwill and, later, with two of the hot-tub borrowers, so I walked up the hill to Radziwill's apartment and phoned Timmy as I went.

I told him I would be home late and that I'd be heading back over to Great Barrington first thing in the morning. I gave him a quick rundown on the cunning liars on whose behalf I was working and on how confused and disgusted I was.

Timmy said, "If they're all so treacherous and underhanded, how come they hired you? They must know that you are reputed to be competent. On that score, word is out."

"Timothy, may I quote you to the Better Business Bureau the next time anybody complains that I'm a screw-up and a con artist?"

"Yes, you can quote me to the Better Business Bureau, the Vatican, and Ellen DeGeneres, too. That's how much I think of your abilities."

"The thing is, these people all seem to want to have it both ways — have somebody on the job who's competent about clearing Fields but incompetent about knowing them and who they are and what they're up to. I keep telling them it can't work that way."

Timmy said, "Maybe they're using you for reasons that will remain unclear until it's too late and you're up to your neck in something heinous and criminal."

"That has occurred to me."

"Be careful."

"I'm doing my best."

"Somebody's already gotten killed in this."

"And hit with a wheel of cheese first."

"Try to avoid both, Donald. Though if you have to choose..."

"Are you going to quote St. Augustine to me again, Timothy?"

"No, I was going to quote my Aunt Moira. 'Keep your priorities as straight as your lipstick.' I heard her say that to my mother one time when I was a kid. It's a bit of Callahan-family wisdom that has always stuck with me."

"But she never said it directly to you?"

"No, but later on she must have been tempted. It's what they were all thinking."

"Well, I'll keep my priorities as straight as Aunt Moira's lipstick, and I'll come home to you un-dead but perhaps smelling vaguely of an overripe Camembert."

"I'll keep my receptors cleansed."

"And you might want to open a window."

□ □ □ □ □

Radziwill had just gotten home from work at Barrington Video and was waiting for me. He opened the door as soon as I buzzed. Josh the waiter/boyfriend had left for work at Pearly Gates, so we were alone in the apartment. Lanky and barefooted in jeans and a T-shirt, Radziwill was confusing to look at with the long tattoo on his forearm with the image of a long arm with an open hand at the end of it. I wondered if he had a picture of an erection on his penis, but asking could have been misconstrued.

Radziwill was tenser than he had been two days earlier and asked if I minded if he smoked a joint, and I said fine. He said he rarely smoked anymore, but he was upset that Barry was in custody. Radziwill had called the lockup, and the cops wouldn't let anyone but his lawyer visit the suspected murderer.

I said, "Were you surprised that Barry was hiding here in Great Barrington?"

He gave me an ironic *oh, honey!* look and said, "*Suh-praaahzed?*"

"Yeah, I figured he was here, and you and probably dozens of others knew it — hundreds, maybe — and I was being kept in the dark for no apparent reason. What was that about?"

Radziwill sucked on his weed. "Barry said don't tell you till you showed you were really on his side. He's still not entirely convinced you aren't reporting to his family. It was my idea to hire you, 'cause you seem okay to me. I'm a more trusting person than Barry is. And Bill checked you out, and you have creds."

"And who is this family of Barry's he thinks I might be in cahoots with?"

"They are *baaaad.*"

"And who and where are these bad people?"

"I'm sorry, Donald, but Barry would have to tell you that. And I don't think he will. It's the one thing he is really pathological about. But you don't need to know; I can promise you that. You can take my word for it, though, that Barry's family is *moooocho* trouble."

I looked at him hard and said, "You know, Bud, you don't talk like the other Kennedys. Is that because you're from the Polish branch?"

Now he laughed. "That's all bullshit."

"Do tell."

He was shaking with mirth. "I made up the name and all that Kennedy hooey."

"It's my impression hardly anybody believed it."

"I know that. I'm not stupid. But I come from a family of conservative wing-nuts who all hate the Kennedys. So when I left that life behind, it seemed like it would be fun to stick it to them — especially my grandfather — by seeming to become everything they despised. Of course, they don't know about it."

"Why haven't you told them?"

"Because," Radziwill said grimly, "I don't want to have anything to do with any of them ever again. To say they hate gay people is putting it *maaaahldly*. I have a new, good life now, and the hell with all of those sad, wretched people."

"Who's your grandfather, Bud? Anybody I'd know?"

He just laughed and took another toke.

I said, "And is Barry's story similar?"

Radziwill nodded. "Similar but not the same. His story is a whole lot more complicated. Maybe he'll tell you about it when this is all over. Or maybe he won't. It's a real horror, and Barry just wants to forget it if he can. Ya know, you and Ramona Furst really have to get Barry out of this totally dumb murder charge thing. It's just so...so *stupid*."

"I'm trying," I said. "I'd work faster and better if everybody was honest with me, the way you've started to be. What about Bill Moore? Is his story like yours and Barry's — fleeing an impossible family situation?"

Radziwill looked puzzled. "No, why? I mean, I don't think so."

"I'm told that Bill is a depressive man with a problematical past."

"Yeah, Bill gets depressed," Radziwill said. "But I'm not sure why. It might be something to do with when he worked for the government. I think maybe he was doing some kind of secret government work, and maybe he had to do some stuff he's ashamed of. Barry never told me about it. He just said don't ask. But I don't think it was family stuff like me and Barry. Bill's a good guy, though, and he and Barry are a good pair. It's great that they're getting married. Where I come from, I never thought I'd see the day."

"Where did you come from, Bud?"

"Out west. I guess you can tell."

"Texas?"

He laughed and shrugged off the question.

"And where did you get the fake IDs? You and Barry?"

He chortled again. "Ain't sayin'."

"Okay then, Bud. Or whatever your name is."

"It actually is Bud. Anyways, that's what I've always been called. I have a real first name, too."

"And is Barry's name really Barry?"

"Noop."

"What is it?"

"Ask him. But don't hold your breath waiting for a straight answer."

"Okay, Bud's-your-real-name. How about this? If Barry didn't kill Jim Sturdivant, who might have? Any ideas?"

Another toke. Radziwill was relaxing now, and I was afraid he would unhelpfully drift away. He said, "Tons of people couldn't stand Jim. But actually *kill* the guy? Jeezum!"

"Sturdivant traded favorable loan terms for sex. Did he work any other scams you're aware of?"

"Not that I know of. I wouldn't know. I never liked the toads, and they never liked me. They're both a couple of phonies. *Were,* in Jim's case."

"What was phony about them that put you off?"

I though Radziwill would talk about the way the toads put on airs and patronized people, but that wasn't it. "Being an imposter myself, I know one when I see one. Those two are fakes from the word go. Especially Jim. He wasn't who he started out to be, I don't think."

"How could you tell?"

"They tried too hard. They were both always playing a part. And I heard once that Sturdivant isn't Jim's real name. Or he had it legally changed."

"From what?"

"Dunno. Older people from Pittsfield might know. That's where Jim was from."

I said, "His obituary will be in tomorrow's paper. That'll have the accurate basic details of his life, we can safely assume."

Radziwill said, "I wouldn't bet on it."

CHAPTER ELEVEN

I met two of the hot-tub borrowers separately after a burger at the Union Bar and Grill on Main Street, and neither was helpful. Mark Berkowicz said the conditions of his car loan from Sturdivant were somewhat embarrassing, but that was all. He was not angry and said he didn't know of anyone else among the borrowers — he supplied an additional name — who might be upset enough with Sturdivant to become violent. Ernest Graves, a comely, sloe-eyed man in his thirties, wasn't even embarrassed by the loan conditions. He likened his multiple hot tub visits to getting a free set of champagne glasses from a bank.

I reached the three other borrowers by phone, and two — Jerry Treece and George Santiago — agreed to meet me the next day. The other, Lewis Bushmeyer, refused to see me and demanded to know who had given me his name. I said Bill Moore, and Bushmeyer hung up on me. He seemed not to want to be associated with the fiancé of a murder suspect, and in similar circumstances neither would I.

I was home in Albany by eleven, fell into bed with Timmy, laughed at Jon Stewart and Steven Colbert, slept uneasily, and dreamed of Batman.

Friday morning, I deposited Bill Moore's check first thing at my bank's neighborhood ATM. I was back in Great Barrington at 7:30 and scanned the *Berkshire Eagle* at a Main Street coffee shop. The Sturdivant murder took up much of the front page, and accompanying the story was a photo of Sturdivant in the company of musicians and officials at Berkshire Opera, one of several arts organizations Sturdivant donated money to. The article told me no more about the crime itself than what I had learned from Trooper Toomey. It said Barry Fields, assistant manager of the Triplex Cinema, had assaulted Sturdivant in Guido's on Wednesday, was now in custody, and was expected to be charged with the fatal shooting that came several hours after the attack in the market. Police said they were uncertain of motive. There was no photo of Fields.

The *Eagle*'s other front-page story — no Darfur, no Iraq — was WILD RIDE FOR MISSY, about a hamster that had survived a journey down the Taliaferro family's malfunctioning garbage disposal. There was an immense photo of the grinning Taliaferros patting a mangled Missy, plus a sidebar story called LUCKY BREAK OR DIVINE INTERVENTION? DO HAMSTERS HAVE SOULS? WHAT DO *YOU* THINK? I recalled Preston Morley's comment that the now-chain-owned *Eagle* had seen better days.

The homicide story provided little personal information about Sturdivant — Steven Gaudios was referred to as Sturdivant's "roommate" — so I located the obituary page in the B section, where Sturdivant got plenty of ink. His corporate career was outlined at length, as was his history as a supporter of conventional good causes. Personal information was sparser. Born in 1939 in Pittsfield, Sturdivant was the son of Anne Marie and the late Melvin Sturdivant. The only survivors listed besides his mother were a sister, Rose Dailey, of Worcestor, and a brother, Michael Sturdivant, of Providence, Rhode Island. Steven Gaudios did not make the cut as a survivor.

There would be no funeral-home calling hours, the paper said, and a private Liturgy of Christian Burial would take place at Our Lady of Mount Carmel Church in Pittsfield on Monday at ten, followed by burial in St. Joseph's Cemetery. Whoever had supplied the obit data to the *Eagle* — probably a family member via the funeral home — had been careful to offer up only the public persona Jim Sturdivant had cultivated and approved of for himself. His public image in death was largely one-dimensional, as it had been in life.

I got directions at the coffee shop — MapQuest would have routed me through New Hampshire — and drove over to Southern Berkshire District Court. The building was an old schoolhouse behind a cemetery. The courtroom was what once had been an elementary school classroom, making it feel like a place for dealing not so much with the felonious as the naughty.

The room's more serious purpose was evident, though, in the manner of the clerks, guards and other attendants, who comported themselves with the gravity appropriate to a murder case. Even the gang at the press table looked less nonchalant than usual. The small courtroom quickly filled up, and I was lucky to find a seat next to Bud Radziwill and his boyfriend, Josh.

"Where's Bill?" Radziwill said.

"Bill Moore?"

"He's not here, and I thought he might be with you."

"He's not."

At ten to nine, a comely, auburn-haired woman in a dark suit and a briefcase that made her list to the right strode in accompanied by a younger woman with her own leather satchel, and they headed for the defense table.

"That's Ramona," Radziwill said. "She'll give Thorny a run for his money. What a jerk he is. This is the DA who once indicted an old lady in Stockbridge for breaking wind in church."

I said, "Was she convicted?"

But Radziwill's attention was now focused on the arrival of the man himself. Thorne Cornwallis and his entourage entered the back of the room with the thuggish invincibility of a presidential convoy of black SUVs, though in fact it was just four guys in dark suits. Cornwallis was a squat man with cold gray eyes and a bad hairpiece, who looked as if he might be happiest standing on a concrete balcony watching his ICBMs roll by. His claque stood while he seated himself at the prosecutor's table. One of them opened the DA's water bottle, then screwed the cap back on lightly.

Barry Fields was led in by two bailiffs. He was wearing his own clothes, but he was shackled and seemed dazed. He did not look at us or anyone else in the room, but as Fields eased into a seat beside Ramona Furst, he suddenly came to life and began to talk animatedly to his lawyer. Furst listened and then wrote rapidly on a pad.

Trooper Toomey ambled in and joined the prosecutors. I asked Radziwill who the other suits were beside and behind Cornwallis, but he didn't know. One, he thought, must be an assistant DA, and the others were "CPCU guys." Radziwill said the CPCU was the DA's investigative arm, the Crime

Prevention and Control Unit. He said, "It sounds East German, but they're local."

Just after nine, Judge John B. Groesbeck made the Mame-like entrance that protocol required, casually instructed everyone to have a seat, and got down to business. Cornwallis was the first to speak, and said the commonwealth was charging Barry Fields with first-degree murder. Cornwallis larded his gaudy presentation with inflammatory adjectives — he called the crime heinous but pronounced it *heen-ee-us* — and reeled off the awful events we had all heard about. He offered no additional evidence, however, that Fields was the shooter. It was all circumstantial and centered on the assault in Guido's, Fields' lack of an alibi that night, and then his running away and hiding.

Fields sat stiffly through the accusations and didn't visibly react until Cornwallis said, "Your honor, given the brutal nature of the crime, the commonwealth is asking for a dangerousness hearing in order to show that Mr. Fields should remain in custody until trial."

At this, Fields leaped to his feet and shouted, "Judge, there's a harmless old lady back there in shackles!"

Furst tugged at Fields' arm to get him to sit down and shut up, but by then the bailiffs were moving toward him fast.

Fields ignored them and continued to shout. "Myra Greene is eighty-nine years old! They've got her back there in chains! I don't care what you do with me, but..."

Judge Groesbeck was instructing Fields to sit down, his lawyer was standing now and pleading with him to cooperate, and the bailiffs had Fields by the arms and were struggling with him and glancing at the judge for guidance.

Cornwallis threw up his hands and said, "Need I say more? This unstable man must *not* be released on bond."

"He's going to indict Myra!" Fields yelled. "Judge, you know Myra! This is insane!"

A grim-faced middle-aged man in horn-rimmed glasses, Judge Groesbeck banged his gavel repeatedly, and when Fields refused again to be seated, the judge ordered the bailiffs to take him back to the lockup. Fields was led away, not resisting, but still shouting about Myra Greene's incarceration.

With Barry out of the room, the judge looked through some papers and said, "Might the defendant be referring to this matter of aiding a fugitive that I'm to hear next? It seems that way." He looked from Cornwallis to Furst and back again. Furst sat shaking her head.

"That would appear to be the case, your honor." Cornwallis said. "Myra Greene aided Barry Fields in his flight from the law. This is, as your honor knows well, a class-B felony. We intend to prosecute Mrs. Greene, and her arraignment is on the docket for this morning."

The judge said, "And you've got her back there in the lockup? This eighty-nine-year-old woman?"

"Judge, the commonwealth does not, of course, plan to oppose bail for Mrs. Greene. We don't see her as a serious flight risk."

"No," the judge said. "Myra Greene on the lam I would have a hard time imagining."

Now Ramona Furst asked to speak. She said she believed that Fields was understandably upset to see his good friend needlessly in chains, and she was sure he would observe courtroom decorum after Mrs. Greene was released.

"Are you suggesting that your client should determine the court's schedule?" the judge asked.

"No, your honor. I'm only trying to do what will work for the court and for all of us."

The judge considered this and said, "Mrs. Greene's case is another matter. I have to say, I'm amazed that it seemed necessary for this eighty-nine-year-old woman to be dragged in here as if she were Khalid Sheik Mohammed. But your client, Ms. Furst, is another case. His recent actions, from his flight to his outburst just now, show that he is not rational and is not in control of himself. So I am granting the commonwealth's request for a dangerousness hearing before I consider any bail request. I'll order that hearing for Monday morning. Meanwhile, Mr. Fields will remain in custody at the County House of Correction. For the record, how will Mr. Fields plead?"

"Not guilty, your honor."

"Monday morning at nine, then," the judge said and gestured for Furst to move on.

I wanted to see what kind of horrors Cornwallis had in mind for Myra Greene, but I needed to talk to Furst, and I followed her and her assistant out the door and onto the courthouse steps while Radziwill and Josh stayed behind. A ragtag mob of print and television newshounds came at her, and I stood aside while Furst declared Fields innocent and the victim of a prosecution based on no evidence at all. She said Fields' flight and courtroom behavior were the actions not of an irrational man but of a rational and justifiably angry young man, and she was sure that the court would agree with her on Monday.

As Furst turned to go back inside, I got her attention and told her I was the investigator Bill Moore had hired.

Furst said, "Where is Bill, anyway? Do you have any idea? I can't get hold of him."

"I don't know, but we should talk. I've been on this for twenty-four hours, and I'm spinning my wheels."

"I'm not getting a whole lot of traction either," Furst said, "thanks in part to a client who won't tell me anything about anybody. He does insist that he didn't shoot Jim Sturdivant, which I happen to believe. But we need to do three things, Donald. Show that Barry could not have done the crime, which won't be easy with no alibi. Show that Barry had no motive for shooting Sturdivant — some bullshit argument over Sturdivant hiring you to investigate Barry doesn't cut it. And, if we can, show who had a better motive for killing Sturdivant. As I see it, that last part'll be your job. Are you up to it?"

"Sure," I said, responding more to an organized, attractive and assured woman's sense of clear mission than to any sense that I had any clue as to what to do next.

"Good," Furst said. "Call me later this afternoon with what you've got, and maybe we can do a late dinner. I'll give you all I know, which is next to nothing."

She gave me her cell number, then headed back toward the courthouse to consult with her volatile client.

I yelled after Furst, "Are you representing Myra Greene, too?"

"She doesn't want a lawyer," Furst yelled back, "but Groesbeck will appoint one. Don't worry about Myra. Thorny may have met his match with this woman." Furst hurried into the courthouse, dragging her briefcase full of bullion.

Curious as I was to witness Myra Greene's arraignment, I decided my time would be better spent concentrating on Jim Sturdivant and deciphering who might have wanted him dead. One of the hot-tub borrowers? That seemed increasingly unlikely, though I was obliged to check them all out. And while nobody I met seemed to like the guy, neither did Sturdivant inspire murderous hatred. Most people just thought the toads were icky. Except for Barry Fields, who despised Sturdivant. The more I saw of Fields and the more I learned about him, the more his raw rage was apparent. What was he so angry about? And could that rage turn even more violent than it had in the cheese section at Guido's? And then there was Man of Mystery Bill Moore. Where had he disappeared to, anyway?

No sooner had I asked myself that question than someone showed up with the answer. A broad-faced middle-aged woman with soft gray eyes that matched her short hair had been seated in the courtroom. Now she came out the door and down the steps and approached me.

"Bud Radziwill tells me you're Don Strachey, the investigator," the woman said. "I'm Bill's friend Jean Watrous. I have a message for you from Bill."

"Let me guess. He can't do lunch."

She smiled. "That's right. How did you know?"

"Bill has a way of missing appointments. Like court dates for his fiancé. Where is he, anyway?"

Her look darkened now. "He's in Washington. He'll be back in a day or two, and he asked me to tell you he'd be in touch. He said for you to just to go ahead with your investigation of Jim Sturdivant. And if you have expenses beyond the retainer Bill has given you, you can come to me."

I said, "What's Bill doing in Washington? Is he checking out other assassins like himself who might have had something to do with the murder?"

Watrous reddened and glared at me. "What do you know about Bill's history?"

I said, "Plenty," thinking the lie might elicit some actual useful information about Moore. Wrong again.

Watrous snapped, "That's horrible! You are just...horrible!" With that, she turned and strode away without another word.

CHAPTER TWELVE

I needed to know more about Moore, but even more than that, I needed to know more about Sturdivant and Gaudios. I waited ten minutes for DA Cornwallis and his claque to emerge from the courthouse. While Cornwallis orated and struck Kim Jong Il-like poses for the TV cameras, I caught Joe Toomey's eye and he came over.

"How's it going, Strachey? Did you catch the real killer yet, like OJ?"

"I'm flummoxed, Joe. I admit it. How about yourself? Have you come up with any forensic or other genuine evidence besides the pathetic circumstantial crap that Thorny is retailing to a credulous public over there?"

"No, but what we've got is good for a conviction. Don't get me wrong, though. If you or anybody else can come up with a better candidate for a two-hour guilty verdict on this, I'm all ears. But you haven't and you won't. I haven't located anybody who really loved Sturdivant except his boyfriend and his mother. But I haven't heard of anybody who hated him enough to kill him either — or would have anything to gain by making him dead."

"Who's in his will?" I asked. "Sturdivant was a wealthy man."

"Half of the estate goes to Gaudios, who's already got some big bucks of his own. Anyway, his bridge-club alibi checks out. The rest of the estate is divided among Sturdivant's aged mother, who gets a million and a half, and then local arts organizations, the state Republican Party, and the local Boy Scouts council."

"There's your answer, Joe. Find out who's in charge of the budget for the Scouts, and see if he's got an alibi for Wednesday night. It's a cunning move on the Scouts' part. Bulk up the treasury, and rid the world of another fag in the process."

He looked at me quizzically. "The Scouts do a lot of good, you know."

"I do know. I used to be one."

"Both of my sons are Scouts. They get a lot out of it."

"Well," I said, "I hope neither of them is gay, or he'd be tossed out on his ass."

Toomey looked at me steadily and said, "One of them is gay. Gary. He's fifteen. He's trying to decide whether or not to come out and challenge the Scouts' national no-gays policy — which the Supreme Court already upheld as being legal, since the Scouts are a private organization. Or, he might stay closeted until he's out of the Scouts, because he enjoys it so much. Whatever he decides to do, I told him, I'll support him. His mother said the same thing. And his brother and three sisters, too."

Never assume. I said, "A lucky kid, your son is."

"It's hard. Pittsfield is a conservative city, strait-laced, historically blue-collar, very Catholic. He goes to church and gets this garbage from the priests. Gary would be smart to wait until he's away at college to come out. That would be easier. But we'll see. He's torn."

I said, "Jim Sturdivant is from Pittsfield originally. Do you know his family?"

"Not really. His mother is Mount Carmel. We're Sacred Heart. And we've only lived in Pittsfield for five years."

I recalled something Preston Morley said, and asked, "Have you ever heard anything about something shady in Sturdivant's family history? Someone who knows Pittsfield said there might be something there."

Toomey shook his head. "Sometimes I think everybody in Pittsfield's got something shady in their past. But that's just a cop's cynicism talking. You see a lot."

I said, "I know you know about Sturdivant's loans-for-sex hobby."

"It's disgusting," Toomey said, and looked ill.

"I'm checking out the borrowers."

"Good for you. If you come up with anything, let me know. I'll be interested."

"But why," I asked, "aren't you looking at other avenues in this? Sturdivant has a long history of all kinds of connections with all kinds of people — corporate, social, charitable, and who knows what all. He was a man who got around and who liked to influence people and events. People I've talked to have used words like *controlling* and *manipulative* when describing Sturdivant. My own experience with him bears that out. This is a guy who could well have made some serious enemies along the way, and you're ignoring that."

Toomey looked as if he was about to choose his words with care. "Two things. One is, Thorny and the CPCU guys like Barry Fields for this. Okay?"

"I see."

"Thorny is both an elected official who never gets less than seventy percent of the vote, and he is very old Pittsfield, very old Democratic machine. This is the reality."

"Uh huh." I glanced over at the DA, still doing his Kim Jong Il act for the cameras.

"The second thing is, I think Thorny is right on this one."

"Nah."

"You're being naïve, Strachey. Fields is plainly unstable. He flies into rages. He once nearly lost his job at the Triplex for getting into a fight with a patron."

"Actual fisticuffs?"

"A man complained about some talkers sitting behind him during a movie. Fields went in and told the people to shut up. They told him to fuck off, apparently, and he blew up and dragged two people outside, a man and a woman. For some reason, the couple took off and didn't press charges, so there's no record of it. But I have witnesses to the incident."

"Yes, he threw those blabby creeps out," I said, "but he didn't shoot them. Even though he probably should have. I would have."

Toomey got on his puzzled look again. "The point is, this is a guy who can lose control and you don't know what the hell he's going to do."

I said, "The person who shot Sturdivant seems to have been in total control of his actions. The act was calculated and it was deadly. It was not somebody losing it and popping off the way you've described Fields."

"Strachey, Fields *told* Sturdivant in front of three witnesses that he was going to get rid of him."

"That could have meant anything," I said. "Get rid of him socially, or something."

This sounded painfully lame as I said it, and Toomey just looked at me for a long moment. He said, "Hey, I know you want to stick up for another gay guy. I appreciate that. And Fields has had some kind of rough time in his life, and you want to see that he gets a break. But you really have to face the facts here. I'm telling you. The guy lost it and killed a man, and now he has to suffer the consequences."

I said, "How do you know he had a rough time in life? What do you know about Fields' life I don't know about?"

Toomey shrugged. "I just meant he was gay, and I know that's not easy. As for who Fields actually is and where he came from, I'm still working on that."

"Yeah, me too."

I thought about asking Toomey if he'd checked out Bill Moore's whereabouts on Wednesday night at nine — or Moore's murky background as possibly some kind of government agent — but decided not to implicate my own client unless and until the facts required it.

Toomey left with the DA's office crowd, and I waited a few more minutes until Myra Greene came out, accompanied by Radziwill and the two friends who had bailed her out. Radziwill helped her extract a cigarette from a pack in her side pocket, and then helped her light it.

"Hey, Donald, I got sprung out of there just in time. I was about to go bonkers in the lockup and start screaming like Jimmy Cagney in *White Heat*."

"I just want you to know I didn't rat you out, Myra."

"I know you didn't, dear. That was Susie Schwartz, whose house I was looking after. But I don't blame Susie either. Thorny went at her with a rubber hose, I'm sure."

Myra sounded game, but she was walking unsteadily and seemed unable to move her neck at all. I said, "Once we get Barry out of this, you'll be okay, too. Don't worry."

"Oh, I'm not concerned, Donald. Now, what time is it? I've got to back get to the theater."

"Don't you want to get some rest first?"

"No, dear, I'll be getting plenty of rest when it's my time for the —" she glanced at her friends and then back at me "— for the big you-know-what."

Then she wobbled away, trailing ash and fumes.

CHAPTER THIRTEEN

The first thing Jerry Treece said was, "Steven is calling in the loans."

"Can he do that? I thought Sturdivant was the lender."

"It's in the contract I signed. If Sturdivant were to die, Gaudios would automatically take over as the lender. And the deal was, the loan could be called in on a week's notice."

"That last part sounds kind of mob-like."

"It seemed like a bargain at the time," Treece said resignedly and sipped from his own Sam Adams as I contemplated mine.

We were in a place called The Brewery just north of town, where the potato skins were as rustic as the decor. Treece was a light-skinned black man in his thirties with a high forehead, a shiny beard and a sedate manner. He worked for a photography restoration company in nearby Housatonic and lived there with his partner, Greg.

Treece said he'd met Sturdivant at the Supper Club and had heard from others that Sturdivant lent money at a below-market rate. Treece had heard rumors of the unwritten conditions of Sturdivant's loans, but he said that that would not have been a problem unless it involved unsafe sex. And when the time came for Treece to collect the car loan he requested, the requirements were minimal and unobjectionable. His biggest problem, he said, was keeping from laughing when the dog had his martini.

I asked, "How much did you borrow?"

"Twelve thousand. But I've been paying it off in big chunks whenever I could, and I'm down to eighteen hundred. So Greg and I can get it together by next week without borrowing somewhere else. It was just kind of a shock, especially after what happened to Jim."

"And Gaudios just phoned you this morning and told you to pay up?"

"He said a registered letter was in the mail, but he was just giving me a heads-up on what to expect."

"For some of the other borrowers, this is probably going to be a real problem," I said. "Did Gaudios say what would happen if you didn't pay the loan off within a week?"

"He used the words 'legal action.' I told him to be cool, that I got the picture and I'd pay up. I told him I was very sorry to hear about Jim's passing, and then Steven got weepy and said he and Jim had been together for forty-six years, and how was he going to live without him? He cried on the phone and said he didn't think he could bear it. Both those guys were a couple of scuzzy characters in a lot of ways, but I do feel sorry for Steven. He's totally devastated. Even people who are not very nice are capable of love, and in their weird way these guys had one of the solidest marriages around."

"I don't think they were married," I said. "In fact, Jim told me they were not — for family reasons, he said."

"They wore matching silver wedding bands," Treece said. "I saw them." He laughed and added, "They were the same design as their cock rings."

"Oh, goodness."

"Maybe they had a non-legal union ceremony and exchanged rings at that time."

"Could be," I said. "Though I think not at Mount Carmel Church in Pittsfield, where Sturdivant's mother is a parishioner. Maybe at their house."

Treece laughed at the idea of a gay union ceremony at Mount Carmel. "I don't think Jim was even out with his family. Steven either. Everybody who was gay knew they were a couple, and so did a lot of other people down here in South County. But Pittsfield is another world. It's a kind of gay pit of shame, where only the bravest of the brave come out. For instance, Jim and Steven gave a lot of money to arts organizations and charities, but they were never listed as joint donors. You'd see their names in theater programs as patrons, but unlike most gay couples these days they were always listed separately. It's a schizoid kind of existence, and it has to take a toll on a person."

I said, "Are you from the Berkshires, Jerry?"

He smiled. "Nope. I grew up in Batavia, New York. Would I have come out there? Noooo way. I was too much of a coward. People who come out in their hometowns are the bravest people in the world. But I'm not one of them. Were you, Donald?"

"Nah."

"It's never too late."

"Yeah, it is. Anyway, I'm from New Jersey, where the ex-governor recently did all the coming out the state will be needing for the next several decades."

"Yeah, I read about that."

"How could you not have?"

Treece asked, "When did you come out, Donald?"

"At Rutgers. It was more of a semi-coming-out. Then I found myself in an official capacity in Saigon — that's a large city in Southeast Asia that's since been re-named."

"Yeah, I've read about that, too," Treece said.

"And I went pretty far back into the closet again. Army Intelligence is not the best place to raise the rainbow banner. I sneaked around a little, formed no real attachments, survived the war, got out of the Army, soon fell in love with a fine woman in the anti-war movement, was married for a while, then figured out who I really was, and started getting it right fast."

"And became a grown-up."

"Often a bumbling one, but a grown-up."

"Have you got a honey?" Treece asked.

"You bet. Timothy Callahan and I have been together for a thousand years, though it doesn't feel like more than a hundred and fifty. We're as comfy and nuts about each other as Al and Tipper Gore. Of course, we have had our Bill and Hillary moments. I will say, he never hit me over the head with a lamp, even when I had it coming. Those early conflicts were over differing sexual mores, as is often the case with both homosexuals and heterosexuals, pertaining mainly to monogamy versus a little variety. Over the years we've hit a happy medium in that department. Now we both go to Paris twice a year and join the over-forty grope at the Odessa Baths, and that pretty much takes care of that biological imperative. There are annoyances and roll-your-eyes or even clutch-your-head differences, of course, but all within the normal range. We're a really interesting many-celled organism, the two of us. And terribly lucky to have found each other. We've got exactly the kind of marriage the anti-gay religious right says is needed for social stability, proving that they are full of slit. We're both proud of that."

Treece said, "Jeez, it sounds just like Greg and me. Except we haven't been together for a thousand years. Just five."

"Mazel tov. Together may you live to be a hundred."

"Are you Jewish?" Treece said.

"No, I was raised Presbyterian. So maybe I should just say, 'Oh, go ahead and have a second lump of sugar with your Earl Grey tea, boys.'"

"Yeah, well, I was raised Baptist," Treece said, "and what the Baptists have in mind for me is a big lump of hellfire. Greg and I attend the Church of Christ in Lenox, which is open and affirming. That's where we had our union. You know, I saw in the *Eagle* that Jim's funeral will be in a Catholic church in Pittsfield. But Steven wasn't mentioned at all. It looks like Jim's family snatched him back from his world of sin and corruption. That must be terrible for Steven. Do you think that's why he's calling in the loans? Maybe being around Berkshire County is now so painful for Steven that he's cutting his ties and just running away."

I said, "Possibly. If so, I should ask him what his plans are."

"So, you don't think Barry Fields shot Jim?"

"No, I doubt it."

"I'm glad to hear that. He's tense, but a good guy, I've always thought. So, who the hell would want to shoot Jim? He was obnoxious but basically harmless. Steven's saying it was Barry. But if it wasn't, I wonder if Steven knows a lot more than he's letting on."

"Me too."

I drove down to Sheffield, and there it was: a Realtor's *For Sale* sign on Gaudios's lawn. It felt precipitous and strange. Sturdivant had been dead for less than forty-eight hours, and Gaudios was not just cutting his ties, but erasing his past, remaking his life.

The crime-scene tape was gone now, as well as the cop cars and reporters, and in the soft late-summer sunlight the big house looked serene, even inviting. The Beemer convertible was parked in the driveway, and I pulled in behind it. A light breeze rattled a few leaves off the maples, which were already starting to turn. The lawn had been freshly mowed, probably at the suggestion of the real estate agent, who would surely want all the cosmetics to be just right to help compensate for any remaining bloodstains.

Knocking on the front door, where Sturdivant had been gunned down, would have felt not just disrespectful but creepy, so I walked around back. The pool and hot tub were deserted. I walked noisily up the back porch wooden steps — I didn't want to startle anybody — and rapped energetically on the screen door. I could see into the kitchen, with its gleaming appliances and a fruit basket with a ribbon around it resting on a granite counter.

Gaudios soon appeared, in crisp slacks and a beige polo shirt bearing its manufacturer's insignia, a small creature that might have been a toad but probably wasn't. Gaudios did not look glad to see me.

"Oh, Donald, why do you keep *tormenting* me? What do you want *this* time? Haven't you caused me enough heartache already? Really!"

"I'm here with condolences, Steven. I saw that you weren't mentioned in Jim's obituary. That stinks."

He made no move to open the screen door, and said glumly, "Oh, that's no problem, no problem at all." He seemed about to add something and then thought better of it.

"So the funeral's Monday?" I asked.

Gaudios's face tightened. "Yes. It is. Now, thank you for your condolences, Donald, but I have a lot on my mind and a ton of stuff to do, none of it the least bit pleasant."

"Will you be going to the funeral?"

At that, Gaudios suddenly trembled, burst into tears, and turned quickly away.

I opened the door, and when Gaudios did not object, I followed him to the kitchen table, where he slumped in a chair, still crying. I took a seat across from him and waited while he uncapped a prescription container, extracted a small white pill with a shaky hand, and popped it into his mouth.

"Would you like some water?" I said.

He shook his head no and gulped the pill down. He seemed well practiced at this.

I said, "So it looks like you've been shut out. That's really rotten."

He snuffled some more and said, "We buried What-Not today. Nell Craigy and two of the girls in the bridge club dug a hole ourselves and put him in it out behind the rhubarb."

"Ah." I wondered about the next owner's cobbler. "Is his grave marked?"

"No."

"But you seem to be planning to move."

Gaudios nodded. "The house is on the market. I can't live here without Jim. I just walk around the house all day looking for him. I can't go near the front door, because I'm afraid I'll find him there on the floor all over again, covered with blood. I can't sleep because I keep waiting for him to come home, hoping he's all right. I have to get out of here as soon as possible. I'll go to our place in Palm Springs for now, for the time being.."

"So, you have a house in Palm Springs. That's nice. Any others?"

"We have *pieds-à-terre* in New York and Paris. I'm selling them all, though. I may pick up something in Fort Lauderdale until I decide what to do."

I said, "You and Jim did well financially, it seems. Are you retired, too?"

"Yes, for some years."

"What did you do, Steven?"

Gaudios wiped his eyes with a cloth napkin. He said, "Consulting, for the most part."

"What did you consult about?"

"Ha! You *name* it."

"Like what? Mineral extraction? Dandruff control? Past-life regression therapy?"

Now he was looking impatient. "Mostly financial services," Gaudios said and looked at his watch. "Oh, God, where has the day gone?"

"I know you've called in some personal loans," I said. "Loans with acquaintances in this area." He looked at me hard.

"I'm trying to determine if any of the borrowers might have been involved in Jim's murder."

"That is absurd!"

"I have five names." I rattled them off. "Were there others?"

"You are barking up the wrong tree, Donald. Yes, Jim and I lent money to a number of friends over the years as personal favors. But that has nothing to do with anything, I can assure you. I know you're determined to get Barry Fields exonerated. But you won't because you can't, and you can't because he is an angry young man who lost control and let his hatred spew out, and he killed Jim over...over nothing!"

"Why," I asked, "did you and Jim hire me to investigate Fields? You both told me it was to keep your dear friend Bill Moore from making a terrible mistake by marrying Fields. But Moore doesn't consider either of you dear friends. He thinks of your actions as outrageous butting in where you don't belong."

Gaudios considered this and reddened. I thought, *Good grief, he may be about to say something truthful.*

He said, "The thing was, Jim didn't like Barry."

"Uh huh."

"He offended his mother."

"His mother?"

"Jim's mother and brother were at the Triplex one time seeing *Star Wars: Episode III Revenge of the Sith.* Anne Marie is hard of hearing, and Michael was telling her what the movie was about. Somebody complained about them talking, and Barry came in and told them to keep it down. He was extremely rude in the way he went about it, apparently. Anne Marie told him she couldn't understand the movie without Michael explaining everything, and how was she supposed to enjoy the movie? Barry told them they were disturbing the other patrons, and he'd give them their money back and they'd have to leave. They thought that was unreasonable — they wanted to see how the story turned out — and they refused to go. Barry lost his famous temper, and he grabbed Michael by the arm, and Anne Marie swung her handbag at him. Somebody called nine-one-one on a cell phone and yelled that the police were on their way. Anne Marie and Michael were humiliated and furious, but not wanting to be in the middle of something that would end up in the *Eagle*, they left. Without even getting the refund they had coming, Anne Marie said."

They disturbed people while watching *Star Wars?* So it wasn't even *The Seventh Seal.*

I said, "Did Barry know the yackers were Jim's mother and brother?"

"No, there's was no point in telling him. Michael and Anne Marie wanted to let it go. They don't like to make a fuss."

"And that was the beginning of some grudge by Jim against Fields?"

"Well," Gaudios said, "Barry *was* known to be some kind of weird character. He made up stories about his past — all that BS about Colorado — and he hung around with that annoying Bud Radziwill. Kennedy cousin, my ass! If Jackie O ever met Bud Radziwill, she'd have him arrested for impersonating a Radziwill."

"Is that a crime in Massachusetts?"

"Now you look here," Gaudios snapped. "I've had just about enough of your smart-ass meddling and insinuations and following me around! I've lived a life of law-abiding taste and elegance, and if you know what's good for you, you'll go back to seedy old Albany and leave us alone to worry about our own problems. Thorne Cornwallis is a man not to be trifled with, and if you get in his way in this, he'll take you apart. Thorne is going to put Barry Fields in Walpole, where he belongs, and if you don't watch your step, you're liable to end up there, also. Now, I've got stuff to do, so please, Donald, take your ugly accusations and just get the frig out of here."

I said, "I didn't accuse you of anything, Steven. Should I have?"

He stood up, stalked to the door, and held it open for me. "Just please go!"

I went.

CHAPTER FOURTEEN

I checked my cell phone to see if Bill Moore had called, but he had not. I was meeting George Santiago, one of the other borrowers, at five, so I headed back toward downtown Great Barrington. I reached Ramona Furst on her cell and asked her if I could visit Fields in jail over the weekend, and she said she would set it up. We made a plan for dinner at eight at an Indian place she said was good.

As I drove up Route 7, I tried calling Lewis Bushmeyer again. The hot-tub borrower who had hung up on me the first time I called was now willing to talk, and he was still angry and upset, but this time not at me.

"Did you say you're working for Barry Fields?" he said.

"I am."

"And not for Steven Gaudios?"

"No. Gaudios thinks Barry shot Jim Sturdivant. Or says that's what he thinks, anyway."

"Are you aware that Steven called in my loan? And probably other people's, too?"

"I heard that, yes."

Bushmeyer said in a shaky voice, "I don't happen to have access to four thousand dollars. And my credit is all shot to hell. I can't go to any commercial lender."

"That's bad."

"I told Steven this, and do you know what he said?"

"What?"

"He said, 'Just. Get. The. Money.'"

"So, he was not sympathetic."

"He said — it's hard to believe this — but Steven said, 'How would you like to have both your legs broken?' Can you believe it?"

I said, "That's not very tasteful and elegant."

"Tasteful and elegant? He talked to me like he was some fucking gangster."

I assured Bushmeyer that I was not a party to any of this and said, "I know of five borrowers." I named them. "Do you know of any others?"

"No, I don't. And I didn't know Bill Moore borrowed money from Jim and Steven," Bushmeyer said. "I thought Bill didn't much like Jim and Steven. And I know Barry couldn't stand them. He always referred to them as the toads. In fact, that name kind of caught on."

"It's my impression that nobody was crazy about Jim and Steven, but their charitable largesse and their generous loan terms won them a certain amount of deference and even social standing."

"People put up with them," Bushmeyer said. "They were part of the scenery in gay Berkshire County. But really an embarrassment to everybody."

I said, "So, speaking of embarrassments — did you visit the hot tub in order to procure your loan, Lewis? I am not one to judge. I'm just fact-gathering."

There was a long pause. "It was humiliating."

"Sorry."

"I am twenty-five years old and extremely handsome, and I am very particular about who I have sex with."

"Good for you."

"I have very beautiful genitals, men say."

"That, too. Or, those."

"And I gave myself over to those two — for money. If my credit had been better, none of this would ever have happened. I am so ashamed. And now I'm paying for my misdeed."

"Good luck getting the money together. But four thousand is not as bad as it could have been."

Bushmeyer said, "You don't have any extra, do you? You sound like somebody I wouldn't be so embarrassed to get into a hot tub with."

"I'm not easily embarrassed, either. But I'm afraid I'm not in a position to be helpful, Lewis."

"Then just — just *fuck you!*" he yelled at me and rang off.

Financial pressures can lead to both recklessness and rudeness, and my heart went out.

I phoned Timmy at his office and described my varied day: Barry Fields' arraignment and his outburst over Myra Greene's needless incarceration by the hard-ass DA; Joe Toomey's warning not to mess with Thorne Cornwallis; Jean Watrous's indignation over my description of Bill Moore as an assassin, after he had run off to Washington or elsewhere for unknown reasons; Jerry Treece's revelation that all the loans were being called in, as well as his description of Pittsfield, the city where Sturdivant grew up and in which he was still closeted, as a "gay pit of shame"; Steven Gaudios's distress over being shut out of the funeral and other final rites for the man to whom he had been effectively wed for forty-six years, as well as Gaudios's goofy story about bad blood over Fields offending Jim's mother by asking her to pipe down during *Star Wars: Revenge of the Sith;* and Lewis Bushmeyer's report on (a) the beauty of his own genitalia and, arguably more importantly, (b) Gaudios's threat to have Bushmeyer's legs broken if he didn't pay up.

Timmy said, "Were there just the five borrowers?"

"I still don't know."

"Maybe there were others, and their loans were called in earlier in the week. And one of them who couldn't pay freaked out and decided to get rid of Sturdivant."

"But," I said, "the loans I know about weren't called in until after Sturdivant was killed, and apparently as a result of his death."

Timmy said, "Well, Donald, I'd say 'apparently' is the operative word there."

"Maybe," I said, "you should come over here and tell me what to think and what to do. And then I can wrap this up in no more than ten minutes."

No reply. I could hear his breathing and smell his Colgate breath.

I said, "Oh, yes. Yes, I am frustrated, and yes, I am pissed off."

"But you're not frustrated with me, are you? Or pissed off?"

"Nuh uh."

"Should I come over after work?"

"Yes. Come for the weekend. Bring me some clothes and my toothbrush and things, will you?"

"Okay. I'll help if I can. But don't snap at me if things don't go your way. I'm not the problem here."

"If I can't snap at you, then who can I snap at?"

"You usually have a list."

"One other thing, Timothy. Bring my nine-millimeter. It's in the bedroom closet."

"Oh. Why?"

"I think Sturdivant and Gaudios might have mob connections."

"Now, that makes me nervous."

"Me too. It's nuts, but there's this talk of leg-breaking — usually a giveaway. Gaudios told me he worked in financial services. That could mean loan-sharking, and I don't mean the kind of loan-sharking Visa and MasterCard carry on legally with the enthusiastic endorsement of their dear friends in Congress. I mean the illegal mob kind. And Sturdivant's family apparently has some kind of shady past in Pittsfield. I've got to check all that out."

"But," Timmy said, "loan-sharking means extortionate interest rates. Sturdivant's rates were actually lower than market. That doesn't sound like the Mafia to me."

"And that's the part of it that's really screwy. But the other thing is, Sturdivant's murder is looking more and more like a mob hit. So, if I'm getting into something here, I just want to be armed and alert."

"Do you think maybe Barry Fields crossed the mob in some way, and they've set him up to take the murder rap?"

"Possibly."

"But what could his involvement have been. He's just some gay-guy, movie-nut, theater employee, isn't he? Is it Fields' mysterious past that might be mob-connected?"

"It could be. But a better bet is, he earned their enmity when he told an old lady to shut up, and this particular old lady was the mother of two men who weren't used to having their mom get dissed."

Chapter Fifteen

I made a plan with Timmy to meet at Aroma, the restaurant where I was to dine with Ramona Furst at eight. Then I called Preston Morley and set up a lunch meeting on Saturday with him and his spouse, David Murano, in Pittsfield. Murano's family was old Pittsfield, and he would likely know something about the nature of the Sturdivant family's alleged shady past.

I called Bill Moore's cell phone and got no answer. I left this message: "Hi, Bill. This is Strachey. Did you work as a mob hit man when you lived in Washington? Or were you some kind of fed going after the mob? Or some combination of both? Clue me in. It would be awfully helpful."

I drove into Great Barrington in a steady stream of weekender traffic. It was Friday late afternoon, and the tourists and second-homers were still restless, even the weekend after Labor Day. I spotted Guido's Market on the left, and the parking lot was jammed. I decided to have a look at the site of the wheel-of-cheese attack, and pulled in.

As I drove around the lot searching for a vacant parking space, a dude in a Range Rover zoomed into a handicap space and bounded out of the car and into the market. He was not handicapped in any visible way, had no handicap sticker, and was wearing about ten thousand dollars worth of clothes. I found a vacant space in a far corner of the lot, parked, and made my way back to the Range Rover. With a ballpoint pen, I let the air out of all four tires. A Guido's bagboy came up to me and asked me what I thought I was doing, and I explained. He said, "Cool," and walked on.

Twenty minutes later, back at The Brewery again, hot-tub borrower George Santiago was another noble-browed attractive fellow of thirty or so, a social worker employed by the state. He had no complaints about beautiful-genital effrontery — or didn't mention them — and he was philosophical about Gaudios calling in Santiago's six thousand dollar loan to him. He had only about thirteen hundred dollars left to pay off, and he said his mother in Connecticut had agreed to lend it to him. I asked Santiago if he knew of other borrowers, and he named Treece but had heard of no others. I asked him if Gaudios had threatened him in any way.

"No," Santiago said. "Steven was actually apologetic when he called. He said he was so upset by Jim's death that he was leaving the area, and that's why he was asking that the loan be repaid. He said it was best if he cut all his ties here. That didn't seem wise to me. He's going to lose all his emotional support systems just when he needs them most."

"I'm not sure Steven had any emotional support systems beyond Jim Sturdivant. That's what's so awful for him. Where did he say he was going?"

"Ibiza. He said he and Jim had a house there."

"Not Palm Springs? He told me Palm Springs."

"No, I know it was Ibiza, because I know the island. My ex and I went there once and enjoyed it."

"So you're single, George?"

Santiago sipped his Coke. "Yeah, I'm actually a little man-shy at this point. I've had four relationships in six years that didn't work out. I seem to have an unfortunate knack for ending up with Mister Wrong."

"I've seen that knack often enough. It's like a pernicious virus that's hard for some men to shake. And a lot of women, too."

"One guy was a boozer," Santiago said. "Two were too young and immature, and one guy was so traumatized and depressed it was sometimes actually physically painful being around him. The depressed guy was almost five years ago, and apparently he's doing better now. You must know him, in fact. It's Barry Fields' boyfriend."

"Bill Moore?"

"We were together for about four months not long after he moved to the Berkshires. But it was heavy going. It's a shame that after Bill pulled himself together and seemed to be doing well, his boyfriend — or fiancé, I guess you could say — has been accused of murder."

I said, "Bill is actually the person I'm working for, to clear Barry. I know of his depression. Did he tell you why he was depressed?"

"That was part of the problem," Santiago said. "He would never talk about it. His depression was so disabling, Bill could barely function. He found a job, and he got through that during the day. But after work he'd drink beer and watch sports on TV, and if he could stay awake long enough we'd make love with this incredible intensity. But that was it. Bill is an attractive man, and I wish things had gone differently with us. But he was just too closed up. And it wasn't just intimacy issues, so-called. The guy really seemed to have been psychically wounded in some horrible way that he could never talk about. It was just so sad."

"Did he talk at all about his life in Washington? That's where he apparently lived before coming to the Berkshires."

"Just in a general way. But I don't even know what kind of work he did. Something official or semi-official. I do know that he gets a retirement pension that's fairly substantial for someone who retired at such a young age — early or mid-forties."

"Did he receive checks in the mail?" I asked.

"For a while, I think. We never actually lived together, but I slept over at his place often enough. I think he went to direct deposit at some point, but I do remember seeing these envelopes from the United States Treasury. And I assumed they were Bill's retirement checks."

"Because they were government checks and they were addressed to William Moore?"

"Yes."

"Did Bill ever say he worked for the FBI?" I asked Santiago.

"No, he never said. If he mentioned his pre-Berkshires life at all — and he seldom did — Bill just said he had left all that behind. He said he wanted to start his life over and get it right this time. He did say that a couple of times. He said coming up to the Berkshires was his chance to do things right and not fuck up this time."

"George, did Bill ever refer to any violence in his past life? Violence that he did, or that was done to him?"

Santiago looked uneasy. "Why? Do you think Bill might have had something to do with Jim Sturdivant's murder?"

"Not necessarily. Anyway, the guy is my own client. I wouldn't be working for him if I thought he was involved in a murder."

Santiago looked at me peculiarly, and if I had been looking at me I would have looked at me peculiarly, too.

He said, "Jean Watrous is the person to talk to about Bill. They were friends in DC, and she's closer to him and knows more about him than anybody, I think."

Something occurred to me, and I wrapped things up quickly with Santiago. I thanked him for his perspective and wished him well paying off his loan to Gaudios in a timely way that would not lead to the need for hospitalization and several weeks in a wheelchair. He didn't seem to know what I was talking about, and he said he wasn't worried.

In The Brewery parking lot, I phoned my FBI contact in Washington. Luckily, he had not left for the weekend — in fact, he said, he'd been working late and on most weekends since 9/11 — and I asked him about an FBI retiree named Jean Watrous. No more then two minutes later, I was told, yes, Jean Watrous was retired from the bureau. She had been an employee, assigned throughout her career to headquarters in Washington, from March, 1969 to January, 2002. I asked if she worked in the anti-mob-activities section of the FBI. My source said, no, Watrous had worked in counterterrorism.

□ □ □ □ □

Timmy said, "You know, your name is Ramona, and we're eating in a restaurant called Aroma. That's almost an anagram."

"Yes," Furst said. "Too bad my name isn't Ramoa. Then it would be an anagram."

"You could change it," Timmy said. "That seems to be what a lot of people do here in Massachusetts. People like Bud Radziwill and Barry Fields, your client."

Furst said, "And if you changed your name from Timothy Callahan to Malb Loovinda, that would be an anagram for what I'm about to order for dinner. God, I'm starved."

Timmy and I looked at each other, and both our lips moved.

Aroma was on Main Street, just south of downtown. We had a booth that was private and remarkably quiet. Great Barrington on Friday night felt like SoHo or the Via Veneto on a weekend, with determinedly jolly diners and shoppers tramping up and down the small town's streets by the hundreds or perhaps thousands. They came from all over, to what Furst said were Great Barrington's many dozens of cafes and restaurants. Twenty years earlier, she said, "ethnic" food in Great Barrington meant pizza. Now, with the tourist and second-home boom, there was Japanese, Indian, Thai, even Finnish, and a couple of places that offered jazz, cocktails, and what Furst described as "high-priced grandmother food."

Before dinner, I had walked over to the Triplex, where the Friday-night throngs were descending on the place like *hajjis* at the Dome of the Rock. I spotted Myra Greene in the lobby surrounded by what looked like outraged and sympathetic admirers. They all but hoisted her on their shoulders and carried her around town like a Mexican saint at Candelaria, Santa Myra de la Cinema. It looked like a crowd that could have hanged Thorne Cornwallis in effigy. Bud Radziwill had told me Cornwallis rarely ventured south of Pittsfield, and I could see why.

In our cozy retreat, Furst said, "This is so nice, eating here, even if we're going to talk business. Shall we share a lamb vindaloo, another meat dish and a veggie dish? Or is either of you vegetarian?"

I said, "Timothy eats nothing that casts a shadow larger than Mount Washington. Otherwise, we're happy carnivores."

"My thirteen-year-old is vegan," Furst said. "It gets complicated in the kitchen. And when I'm in a place like this, I tend to pounce on the odd steer or fowl running loose and plunge my fork into it."

Timmy said, "You must be good in a courtroom."

"I am," Furst said. She was still in her courthouse dark business outfit, and she hadn't unwound all the way, despite the dent she had made in her whiskey sour.

I said, "You have kids. And a husband too?"

"Two kids, Jessica, thirteen, and Howie, eleven. My ex has them this weekend. They're great. It makes some other things about the marriage okay to forget about."

I saw now that Furst's lustrous auburn hair might not have been nature's own shade, and I wondered why most women who colored their hair usually looked fresh and new, and men who did it, no matter who they were, usually came across as Dick Clark.

Timmy said, "How long were you married, Ramona?"

"Too long," she said and caught the eye of the waiter, a somber man of late middle age who looked as if he could have been a professor of accounting in Jalalabad. We ordered an assortment of zesty savories.

"Thanks for turning over your Friday night to us," I told Furst. "To us and to Barry Fields. I'm sure you'd rather be out on a date, taking your mind off all this."

"I'm actually not dating right now," Furst said. "I'm just coming out of a relationship with a woman who was too high maintenance, and I'm taking a break from all that."

Timmy said, "Oh, you're gay?"

"Bi," Furst said and dipped a celery stick in some tamarind sauce. "I like men, too, if they meet certain criteria."

"Like, if they have large breasts?" Timmy said jocularly, and to my relief Furst laughed.

"No, Timothy. I go for men with really nice asses. Like Don's here. You're a little skinnier than I generally go for. But you are pretty cute otherwise."

"Timmy's bi, too," I said. "Bipolar. Would that do?"

"Been there, done that," Furst said. "No, what I look for in a man is a shred of decency. And it constantly amazes me how often I find it."

"Why is that so surprising?" I asked gingerly.

"Too many men are so *angry*. It's as if they resent not being able to spend their time roaming the forests spearing things. It's women who more often have reasons to be mad as hell, but most women take life as it comes. It's always a relief to find a man who's like a woman in that regard."

"But has an ass like Don's," Timmy said.

"Now you're talkin'."

I said, "Your client seems to be one of those angry men. Barry Fields is full of rage, but I don't think it's because he isn't allowed to go hunting."

"No," Furst said. "And it's not the anger of a gay man who's still stewing over being forced to conform and date Debbie Dewdrop in junior high. It's more than that. I don't know exactly what Barry's problem is, but I feel certain he came out of some horrendous family situation."

"He won't talk about it to anybody," I said. "Except apparently Bill Moore and Bud Radziwill. Have you heard from Moore?"

"No. There was just a message he left in my office saying he'd be back in town for the dangerousness hearing on Monday. I asked Radziwill about Barry's anger after the altercation in Guido's on Wednesday — I was looking for some mitigating circumstances for the blow-up — and Bud just said Barry's whole family is like that, and Barry is actually the calmest, least dangerous person in his whole brood."

"Where did the two of them meet?" I asked. "Bud the phony Kennedy cousin has his own mysterious past, and I wonder if the key to Barry's troubled history lies with Bud's."

"They met in college or just before college," Furst said. "Bud told me that much. When I asked him where that was, he just said 'the Emerald City,' and laughed. He wouldn't tell me any more. Bud would only say that they weren't wanted by the law anywhere, and not to worry about that."

Timmy said, "They must have followed the yellow brick road."

We looked at him.

"To the Emerald City."

I said, "I'll bet you're right, Timothy. But what does that mean? As a practical matter."

He looked blank. He brightened then and said, "Maybe they're from Kansas."

"Bud sounds as if he's from Texas," I said.

"So maybe they didn't follow the yellow brick road. They took I-10."

Our assorted meat platter arrived, and we helped ourselves to the aromatic morsels.

Furst told me she had arranged my visit with Fields at the Berkshire County House of Correction in Pittsfield Saturday morning at ten. "But," she said, "I'm not sure what you're going to get out of Barry that'll be of any use. He claims not to have known Jim Sturdivant well enough to have any idea who would want to kill him, and I tend to believe him. Sturdivant and Gaudios were both icky guys, but the kind that inspire annoyance rather than homicide. I take it you've checked out the guys who borrowed money from Jim at below market rates in return for blowjobs. Anything there?"

Timmy examined his mint sauce. I said no, I hadn't come up with anything, except Gaudios, as co-lender, had called in the loans within the last two days, and this had upset some of the borrowers. I said, "Ramona, doesn't Sturdivant's murder look to you a bit like a mob hit? I'm talking methodology."

She said, "It does. I wondered about that."

"What do you know about Sturdivant's background? I mean, before he became a precious Sheffield homosexual."

"I don't know anything, really. He's from Pittsfield. I grew up in Lowell. I came out here to be a post-hippie and somehow ended up in law school. So Pittsfield is relatively new to me. And Gaudios is from...where?"

"Springfield, someone said."

"A sad town. Pittsfield is an old industrial city that's trying to make a comeback with cultural tourism and the quality of life that comes with the natural surroundings. Springfield is an old industrial city that's been sinking for decades and has nothing to grab on to. Gaudios is lucky to have fled when he did."

I said, "I want to check out if Sturdivant and Gaudios might have had mob ties. Unlikely as that sounds. They used lending money not for profit but for sex with otherwise unattainable attractive men — a kind of ugly twist on loan-sharking. The murder looks like a gangland hit job. And Gaudios told me he made his money in what he called financial services, though he was adamant in not explaining to me what that meant."

Furst said, "Half the people in the United States work in financial services now. It's what the country produces these days instead of widgets."

"And the other thing is," I said, "Sturdivant's family in Pittsfield has some kind of shady past. I'm going up there tomorrow to find out what that's all about."

Timmy said, "Why wouldn't the DA have thought of that? He's there in Pittsfield, and he must know about any organized crime that goes on."

Furst reached for her drink and finished it off. She said, "Thorny would know about such things, yes. But Thorny is a man in love with the obvious. Or what's obvious to him, anyway. And what's now obvious to Thorny is, the Sturdivant murder is an unfortunate spat involving a couple of South County fags."

I said, "Might I convince him otherwise?"

"You could try," Furst said. "But you'd probably have to drag in the actual mob contract man to do it. That sounds risky, Don. Probably impossible."

Timmy said, "Anyway, you're probably imagining all that mob stuff. The Mafia is a dying institution. Black gangs have taken over the mob's most popular function, keeping a sizable percentage of the population narcotized. The mob in this country exists mainly on HBO now, doesn't it, Ramona?"

She said, "No, not really. They're actually still around," and we all wondered what that could possibly mean in a place as sweetly benign as the Berkshires seemed to be.

CHAPTER SIXTEEN

The Berkshire County House of Correction was off a main highway a few miles north of Pittsfield, near a shopping mall and a cement plant. The place was on the new side, with the let's-not-overspend look of something put up by the Army Corps of Engineers in New Orleans — or maybe an especially brutal high school. A light drizzle was falling Saturday morning just before ten, a bummer for the weekenders in Great Barrington but probably no loss to the men and women who had been locked indoors for having behaved incorrectly, or for seeming to Thorne Cornwallis to have done so.

I went through the security rigmarole — multiple ID checks, heavy metal doors opening and closing electronically — and was led eventually to a small room with a window to a corridor where corrections officers were stationed. I sat on one side of a metal conference table, and Fields was led in and left alone on the other side.

He looked awful. His blue eyes were bloodshot and his red lips dry. Fields' orange jumpsuit was a size too big for his mid-sized frame. He was subdued, as if he were resigned to spending the rest of his life in this building, even though no matter what happened he would not. Fields had a bruise on his left temple, and I asked him about that.

"Did you get hit? You're bruised."

A wan shrug. "An inmate. Last night I tried to change the TV to the Independent Film Channel."

"And somebody preferred Bill O'Reilly?"

"No, sports."

"The inmates are learning about fair play. This is good, maybe."

"Not fair play. Jumping on people." He said, "I appreciate your coming here."

"Glad to help. I'm getting paid. And in some weird way, I may have set all this in motion. I mean, myself and Jim

Sturdivant and Steven Gaudios. So I have to get you out of this."

Fields said listlessly, "Yeah, that would be good."

"You didn't shoot Sturdivant, did you?"

"No."

"But you did hit him with a large cheese."

"He had it coming," Fields said. "I know, I know. Assault is assault. And I don't believe in violence. In Guido's that day, I just lost it. I do that sometimes, as you have no doubt heard. Apparently it's congenital, not that that's any excuse."

"What did Sturdivant say that set you off?"

"He...well, he insulted my mother."

"Uh huh."

"The funny thing is, my mother is a horrible human being."

"How so?"

"I was reacting to the fact that what he said about her is all true. When I heard it, I just blew up."

"Understandable. What did Jim say?"

"Anyway, he didn't even *know* my mother."

"He didn't?"

"How could he? Or at least there's no way he could know that the woman who is my mother is my mother."

I said, "Is your mother a well-known criminal?"

This produced a little slit of a smile. "You could say so, I do believe. The mother stuff started because Jim said I had offended *his* mother. Of course, I didn't know what the fuck he was talking about. It turns out — he told me in Guido's, and I remembered — that I had once told her and Jim's brother to be quiet during a movie. They'd been bothering other people in the theater."

"I heard about this incident," I said.

"So when they wouldn't shut up, I made them leave. They were really obnoxious about it. The guy — it was Jim's brother, I now know — threatened to have somebody break my legs. The guy was a total thug."

"He used those words?" I said. "Somebody was going to break your legs?"

"Yeah."

"And did anybody? Break your legs, or retaliate in any way?"

"No, the guy and the old lady just left in a hurry. This was after somebody called the cops. A Great Barrington cop arrived just as they were leaving, but they seemed to want to drop the whole thing and just get the hell out of there, which they did do."

Outside the window, two officers led an unshaven young man in manacles down the corridor. Fields noted this somberly, as did I.

I said, "Have you ever been in jail before, Barry? Or whatever your real name is."

He looked back at me and said, "No. I'm the first in my family to be incarcerated. Ironical as that may be."

"Are you going to tell me now about your family situation? My impression is, it's dreadful."

His gaze was steady. "No, I'm not going to tell you about my family. Not now, not ever."

This was getting annoying. Fields bore no resemblance to Pol Pot, or to Ayman al-Zawahiri, or to George W. Bush's recently retired secretary of the interior, Gale Norton. I said, "How come you won't tell me? I can keep my mouth shut."

"Because that was then, and this is now. I'm not the same person I was before. That person is essentially dead, and to me so are all the people from that dead life. So just drop it. Because if you keep asking about my past life, you will be wasting your breath."

I said, "What did Sturdivant call your mother?"

"He didn't really call her anything. He just said I had insulted his mother, who was a refined Christian lady. He said next to his mother, my mother was probably an unholy screaming bitch."

"And that struck a chord?"

Fields let himself smile. "I had to pay for the cheese. Two hundred eighteen dollars. I didn't even get to keep it. It's probably down at the Great Barrington police station. The Barrington cops are eating fine Italian cheese with their Dunkin' Donuts."

I said, "Witnesses at Guido's said you threatened to kill Sturdivant. And the night before, you even told me you were so mad at Jim you were going to get rid of him. What is anybody supposed to make of that?"

Fields lowered his head. "I know I said that. That's so awful."

"But you didn't mean it."

He looked up at me now and said, "That's what my mother and father used to say to me when I was bad. They said they were going to get rid of me. Or they were going to kill me, because I didn't deserve to live. It's hard to believe, I know."

"Well."

"And I sort of picked up that habit, apparently. Along with my family's anger. It's a problem," Fields said, indicating the prison bars next to him.

I didn't really know how to respond, and Fields seemed ready to move on. So I said, "What about Bill Moore?"

"What about him?"

"Where is he?"

"He's helping you out, he told me."

"Well, he didn't tell me that. He's gone — gone to Washington, according to Jean Watrous."

"Then you can believe it. Jean would know."

"But how can Bill be helpful to me in Washington?"

Fields considered this. "Bill knows people there who can probably give him information about Jim Sturdivant. Okay? Just be patient, Donald."

"Is Bill a former mob wiseguy?"

He laughed. "Jesus, no."

"He told me he worked for the FBI. But I checked. No William Moore fitting Bill's description ever worked for the FBI. So, what's the story, Barry?"

After a moment, Fields said, "The thing is... Well, actually... Bill changed his name, legally."

"After he left the bureau?"

"Just after."

"How come?"

Fields stared at the table and did not reply.

I said, "Did the bureau help him change his identity? Was it their idea?"

Fields shook his head once. "No."

"He changed his name on his own?"

"You'd have to ask Bill about that," Fields said. "It's something that he wants to keep private." He looked straight at me, poker-faced, and waited.

I said, "Bill changed his name. You seem to have changed your name. Bud Radziwill seems to have changed his name. There must be something in the water in Massachusetts. Maybe Myra Greene is really Suzanne Rockett, and Thorne Cornwallis is actually Duncan N. Cadwallader. And before I leave the state I will have turned into somebody else too. What the hell is this all about, Barry, this business of just about everybody involved in this weird, ugly mess wearing masks?"

"We all have our reasons," Fields said.

"Oh, you do."

"You better believe it."

"I might believe it if I only knew exactly or even approximately what it was I was supposed to believe."

Fields looked at me with what I took to be pity. "Look," he said. "My family are monsters. I'm ashamed of them. Bud feels the same way about his. So, please. Just drop all that. I understand why you're frustrated and confused, Don. But just try to understand. And Bill...well, he did something he's ashamed of, and he's trying to forget it. Not to forget it — he never can. But just to not have it *coming up* all the time. *Okay?*"

I said, "Could any member of your family have been involved in Sturdivant's shooting?"

Fields looked startled. "They don't know where I am. Or even who I am."

"How can you be sure?"

He shuddered. "Anyway, they don't go around shooting people. They don't have to."

So, what were Fields' horrible family? Third World arms merchants? The Ceaușescus of Romania?

I said, "You told me yourself, Barry, that you were afraid that your family had found you. When you discovered that I was checking up on you, you thought it might be your family I was working for. Maybe somebody from wherever you came from did track you down. And set you up for the Sturdivant murder. Is that how your family operates? Your loathsome, despicable family?"

Fields slumped. "I wish."

"You wish what?"

"That they were that subtle."

"I want to pursue this. Along with other angles, including a possible mob-hit scenario."

"My family are not gangsters. That I can guarantee you," Fields said and rolled his eyes toads-style.

"But maybe Jim Sturdivant's family has mob ties. This I'm about to look into."

Fields said, "I guess that's what Bill might have meant."

"What did he say?"

"He said he wanted to talk to some people and look at some computer files that might have something on Sturdivant's father and brother. Something at the Justice Department. Bill still has friends there. I met some of them once. They're not as hard on Bill as he is on himself. Most of them aren't, anyway."

I wondered about something. "Barry, if Bill is onto what he thinks might be a mob connection to Sturdivant's murder, why doesn't he just pursue that himself? Why spend money on me? Why bring me into it at all?"

"Because," Fields said without hesitation, "I don't think he wants to solve the murder. He wants you to do it."

"Why?"

"If he solves the crime, people will wonder how he did it and ask a lot of questions about Bill's past. And that is exactly what he doesn't want to happen. But if you solve the crime, he can resume his life as William Moore and I can resume my life as Barry Fields. It will be almost as if nothing ever happened."

"What's your real first name? Does it start with a *B*?"

Fields smiled. After a moment, he said, "Benjamin."

"Do you and Bill call each other by your real names sometimes?"

"Yes. Those are our affectionate names for each other. Our former names. We use them when we make love, and other times too, sometimes, when nobody else is around."

"And does your former last name start with an *F*?"

Fields grinned again. "Nope."

"Barry...I mean Benjamin..."

"No," he said, "you have to call me Barry. That's really who I am now. To you, and even to myself. I really have reinvented myself, Donald, and you have to respect that. As for my family, and any possible connection to Jim's death, I'll have to think about that. If it makes any sense at all, I'll tell you what you'd have to know to check it out. But I have to say, I doubt that's the answer. These people are worse than mere homicidal maniacs. And if you never have to get anywhere near them, be grateful. Just be grateful for that."

"I hope I don't have to meet them, Barry. But you should know, I will do what I have to do to get you out of here."

Fields suddenly teared up and looked away from me. In a thick voice he said, "Good. There's no time to waste. This place is starting to get me down."

CHAPTER SEVENTEEN

I met Timmy at the Starbucks where I'd dropped him off in a shopping center down the road from the jail. He was going at the *Times* crossword puzzle, all his mental resources cocked, loaded and firing sporadically. To see Timmy attack the Saturday or Sunday puzzle was like watching Washington commanding his troops at Yorktown. Timmy was barely aware that I had entered the coffee shop, and while he dealt decisively with some linguistic threat on his left flank, I looked over the day's *Berkshire Eagle*.

The Fields arraignment made page one, with a color photo the size of a beach blanket above the fold showing Fields being led into the Great Barrington courthouse. A smaller picture of Cornwallis bloviating on the courthouse steps bore the caption "DA Thorne Cornwallis called the murder of a Sheffield man on Wednesday 'heinous.'"

The accompanying story contained no new information, but the reporter had dug up several witnesses to Barry Fields' assorted outbursts of temper. One woman said she had seen Fields "drag an old lady" out of the Triplex one time for talking. The old lady was not named. A separate story on Myra Greene's indictment on harboring-a-fugitive charges centered on the popular local woman's overnight incarceration. Three of Greene's friends said this time Cornwallis had gone too far and he would surely pay at the polls in November. There was a photo of Greene in chains entering the courthouse, an unfiltered cigarette dangling from her lips.

Timmy gradually became aware that he was in a room with other people, one of them me, and I described my visit with Barry Fields. I said I was pursuing two angles now, the mob-hit possibility, and the long-shot chance that some member of Fields' horrible family had set him up.

Timmy said, "How can you look at Fields' family when you have no idea who they are?"

"I might be able to persuade Moore or Radziwill to tell me who Fields really is — or used to be, as he thinks of it — if I can convince them it will help get Fields out of this fix he's in. Or maybe Jean Watrous can be brought around — even though I did not win her over with my characterization of Moore as an assassin. That really sent her into a swivet, and I wish I knew why."

"Maybe because it's true."

"I doubt it. Fields just told me Moore really did work for the FBI, but changed his name when he left the bureau and moved up here. If it had been the CIA, I'd have to wonder what violence he might have perpetrated in the name of Jesus and George Tenet. But post-Hoover-era FBI agents tend to be law-abiding citizens. One possibility, of course, is that Moore killed somebody accidentally, and that's the source of his terrible shame and regret. Anyway, Fields says Moore is in DC digging into Sturdivant's family now, so we'll see how that goes."

Timmy said, "Maybe you could find out who Fields used to be by ID-ing his fingerprints. It's old-fashioned and low-tech. But I'll bet it would work."

I helped myself to a sip of his tepid latte. "Maybe. I could easily get his prints on something. And now the Great Barrington cops must have his prints on file too, if I could get hold of them."

"And your old flame Lyle Barner at NYPD could run the prints through the national data center."

"The DA here has probably had Fields' prints checked. Anyway," I said, "it's possible Fields — or whatever his name used to be — was never fingerprinted. If he was never arrested or never served in the military or worked for the government, he might not have been inked."

"Sometimes elementary school children are fingerprinted now. Though you have to wonder if Fields' family would have allowed that. Anyway, maybe to the rest of us Fields' allegedly vile family wouldn't seem so rotten. Maybe they're just eccentric."

"No, Radziwill knows about Barry's family, and he told me they are truly wicked. Much worse than his own family, he said, and apparently the not-really-Radziwills are bad enough. And Moore doesn't dispute it either."

Timmy said, "I wonder what the Republican family-values crowd would make of Fields' family."

"Maybe they'd approve. They're often pretty daffy."

"Or maybe the Republican family-values crowd *are* Fields' family."

"Don't think that hasn't occurred to me."

"Li'l Barry Falwell."

I said, "Timothy, I want you to go to Virginia and get me a sample of Jerry Falwell's DNA."

"Okay. Will a strand of hair be okay?"

"No, I want one of his jowls. Or a couple of hemorrhoids. Are you up to it?"

"As soon as I check my appointment book. I have a busy schedule."

"Meanwhile, let's have lunch with somebody who might actually be forthcoming with useful information instead of acting cagey and evasive."

Timmy said that sounded refreshing.

□ □ □ □ □

Preston Morley and David Murano lived in a pleasant, maple-shaded, two-family Edwardian frame heap on Gordon Street, not far from Pittsfield High School. Their side of the house had a yard sign for a candidate in the upcoming primary election, and the other side of the house had a sign for another candidate. The non-Morley–Murano section of the house also had a sign in the window that read *Jesus is Coming Soon*. It felt a little like Sunnis and Shias trapped in the same dwelling, though as Timmy and I walked up the porch steps a middle-aged woman emerged from the Shia side and offered a smile and a hearty "G'morning."

Morley greeted us on the Sunni side and led us through rooms full of theatrical posters and memorabilia to the kitchen, where we met Murano, who was fixing lunch. He was large and dark-eyed, with a bushy black mustache, and the nimbleness of the dancer Timmy said he once had been. Morley, Timmy's old classmate, was, like Timmy, not much changed from their track-and-field Georgetown days, except for their matching extensive bald spots. They chortled over their missing-hair situations, and Morley led us to the back porch, where a table had been laid with cheery care, including a centerpiece of many-colored nasturtiums from the flower garden below us. Here was the Massachusetts gay-marriage hell over which much of the nation was at that time clutching its head and recoiling in horror.

Once the gazpacho and green salad were served, and a few mildly racy Georgetown stories retold, Murano said, "I guess you want to hear about my cousin."

What was this? "Your cousin?"

"Jim Sturdivant was a distant relative of mine. Though I hardly knew him. He was older, and anyway he left Pittsfield when he went to college, and he was really pretty much a South County second-homer until he retired. And even then he didn't set foot in Pittsfield a whole lot, I don't think."

Morley added, "Miss Jimmy apparently would not have been welcomed by the other Sturdivants, who suspected that he was maybe a little bit *that way.*"

"Not that Jim's that-way-ness was ever spoken of in the family," Murano said.

I said, "It sounds as if Jim didn't even speak of it himself, his being gay."

"Within his circle of gay friends, yes. Outside that circle, never. I met a Whitney Defense Systems gay guy one time when I knew Jim was their company spokesman, and I asked the guy if he knew Jim. He did, and he was surprised to hear that Jim was gay. And he didn't know anything about Steven, even though Jim and Steven had been together since college. It's really sad, but I understand it because I grew up in Pittsfield too."

Morley said, "Pittsfield is the Paris of the Berkshires. Too bad it's Paris, Illinois."

Timmy said, "It's a very pretty old city. I can see that part of its beauty, however, is its many fine Catholic churches. I know too well what that can mean."

"It's a priest-ridden old blue-collar city," Murano said. "I still love the Catholic church for its esthetics and the decent parts of its morality and its history. And in some parts of the world the church is actually a force for social justice. But the church's ideas on sexuality are soul-destroying, and Pittsfield is a poisonous place to grow up if you're gay. Jim Sturdivant got out when he could, but not before he became so terrified and ashamed of his sexuality that it made him kind of bonkers — schizoid and twisted and with some kind of need to control and humiliate other gay men."

Morley said, "I told David about Jim's unusual lending practices."

"How come you survived Pittsfield?" Timmy asked Murano. "I saw the rainbow sticker on your car, and I take it you two were licensed to be married at Pittsfield City Hall."

"Let me explain," Morley said, "just how unusual my husband is. David was the first teacher in a Pittsfield public school to come out, and that was twenty years ago. He was hugely popular and indispensible, so that helped. But this was before there were any serious legal protections, so it was a brave and gutsy thing to do. Not many gay teachers here are out. Either they're afraid a bigoted parent will complain, and the school committee will be too gutless to back them up. Or they're infected with the same shame and embarrassment Jim Sturdivant lived with. But far more are casually out now than was the case when David came out, and I just admire the hell out of them. The bravest people I know are gay men and women who stay in hometowns like Pittsfield where they grew up and simply refuse to live lives of secret shame and humiliation."

Timmy said, "I never came out in Poughkeepsie. I snuck around until I got out of town."

"I barely managed to come out in college," I said. "Never mind back home."

"I could never have done it back in West Gum Stump," Morley said. "My Little League coach would have called me queer."

Timmy said, "I didn't know you played Little League, Preston. You never told me that. It's not how I ever thought of you."

"I'd go to ball practice and then go home and play my Ethel Merman records. This was known about me."

Timmy said, "Ah, there's my Preston."

"In Pittsfield," Murano said, "you would have kept your Ethel Merman habit carefully concealed. Or paid a heavy price. Or been afraid you would."

Timmy raised a glass of limeade, and the rest joined in when he said, "To Pittsfield's bravest!"

"Hear! Hear! To Pittsfield's bravest!"

"And then," Murano said, setting his glass down, "in Jim Sturdivant's case, there was this other problem."

"It being?" I asked eagerly.

"Some of his family were criminals."

"Uh huh."

"Not just criminals, but the organized crime type. The old mainly Italian mob is pretty much out of the county now. It's black gangs from New York that deal drugs. But when I was growing up — and especially when Jim was young — there was the numbers racket, card games, protection, some prostitution, and the big one, racetrack betting. There's still some of that that goes on, a lot of sports betting especially."

Timmy said, "Not to be too careless with an ethnic stereotype, but Sturdivant doesn't sound to me like much of a Mafia family name."

Murano said, "No, but Murano does."

"Jim changed his name?"

"Phil Murano, Anne Marie's first husband, was Jim's father. The guy was a low-level mob goon. He was convicted in a loan-sharking crackdown in the late forties and was sent to Walpole, where he was stabbed to death in a brawl in 1951. Anne Marie married Mel Sturdivant a couple of years later, and she changed her name and the kids' names to Sturdivant."

Timmy said, "Loan-sharking. Hmm."

"Jim had a hard time growing up," Murano went on, "because people in Lakewood — the neighborhood over near the GE plant where we all lived then — knew his real dad was a mobster. Some people held it against him and Michael and even Rose, and other people took the other tack and expected Jim to be a tough, mean guy too. Which very definitely was not in the cards. Jim was choir and drama club material and a disappointment to both the Muranos and Sturdivants who were into sports and heavy betting. Luckily, Michael turned out to be 'all boy,' as I remember my mother's aunts calling him, so that took some of the pressure off Jim. But Jim went off to UMass right after high school, and he never really came back to Pittsfield to live. Also, he met Steven in college, and back then neither the Muranos nor the Sturdivants would have put up with *that*."

I said, "None of this is mentioned in the newspaper obit. I don't mean the mob stuff or the gay thing. But the omission of the legal father seems odd."

Murano laughed. "The family provides that type of information to the funeral home, which gives it to the paper. Anne Marie, Michael and Rose apparently chose to leave it out. And since the *Eagle* was bought by a penny-pinching chain, turnover has been so high that the paper has no institutional memory. You could list Ma Joad as one of somebody's survivors on an obit form, or Buffalo Bill Cody, and some hapless kid working for minimum wage over there would just type it up."

"I said, "David, tell me more about the brother, Michael. The one who was 'all boy.'"

"I don't know that much about Michael. He's five or six years younger than Jim was — Rose is in between — and he left Pittsfield a long time ago. The paper said he lives in Rhode Island. That's all I know, really."

"Apparently Barry Fields once threw him and Anne Marie Sturdivant out of the Triplex movie house for bothering other patrons, and Michael threatened to break Fields' legs. Do you know this story?"

"No. Wow. Break his legs?"

"And Steven told one of the hot-tub borrowers who resisted repaying his loan ahead of schedule that he might just have his legs broken if he didn't pay up. It's a uniquely mob-like way of interacting with people, and in this extended family, leg-breaking threats seem to trip off people's tongues with unusual ease."

Morley said, "I hope this isn't like Chekhov's gun on the mantelpiece, which, if it's visible when the curtain rises, has to go off before the curtain goes down."

"That has to do with the audience's dramatic needs," Timmy said. "I for one do not feel the need for any leg-breaking. I don't even like noogies."

I said, "And there are several features of Jim's murder that look a lot like a mob hit. Is it possible that Sturdivant only seemed to recoil from his gangster-father background, and that he was in fact into something illegal with or without his brother? He kept his being gay rigidly compartmentalized. Maybe he had yet another aspect of his life that he kept secret. And Steven knows about it, and is happy to see Barry Fields take the rap for the killing so that none of this whatever-it-is comes to light?"

Everyone at the festive table looked unnerved by this possibility.

Murano said, "I don't know why Jim would have been mixed up in anything truly criminal. He made tons of money legitimately. Why would he do it?"

"To connect with the memory of his real father?" Morley asked. "Stranger things have happened, psychologically speaking."

"And," Timmy said, "we know Jim was so uncomfortable with being gay that he never publicly acknowledged his relationship with Steven. Maybe he became a mob guy because it was butch. A diversionary tactic not to throw off the general public, but for...whose benefit? His brother? His mother?"

"The Sturdivants and Muranos all knew Jim was gay," Murano said. "It was just never spoken of. As long as Jim didn't flaunt it — that is, mention it north of Great Barrington — the façade of churchy hetero respectability was maintained. And that's what really mattered to Anne Marie, I'm sure. She could tell the girls at Mount Carmel bingo night that her middle-aged son Jimmy just hadn't met the right girl yet."

I said, "Who would be in the best position to know about current Berkshire County mob activities and whether or not any Muranos or Sturdivants might be involved?"

Murano and Morley looked at each other somberly and nodded. Murano said, "Thorne Cornwallis would be the person to talk to. But we really would not recommend that."

"Why not?"

They just sighed and shook their heads.

CHAPTER EIGHTEEN

"This is bullshit, total crap! I have never heard such lame-brained, dickhead, idiotic crap, and believe me, I've heard it all!"

Thorne Cornwallis was livid, in the clinical sense, his blocky face crimson. I watched to see if his hairpiece would twirl, cartoonlike, on a propeller pin, but it only bobbed a few times.

I was seated across a cluttered desk from the DA in his office near the Berkshire County Courthouse. The third-floor office overlooked Park Square in the center of Pittsfield. The square was actually an oval, a heavily traveled, multi-laned traffic rotary with grass, trees and a Civil War monument in the middle. My attention went back and forth between Cornwallis sputtering and flailing his arms a few feet from me and the bumper-car mayhem down below.

I had called the DA's office hoping to set up an appointment for Monday, but Cornwallis himself happened to be alone in the office and picked up the phone. When I told him I was working for the Fields defense and had a mob-hit angle I wanted to pursue, Cornwallis let fly with a string of obscenities and then said he would give me ten minutes before he had me run out of town. Timmy remained at the Morley–Murano den of gay-marriage perdition while I went off for some face time with Berkshire County's head prosecutor.

"Jim Sturdivant was about as likely to be whacked by the mob as Elton John would be," Cornwallis told me, waggling a be-ringed, well-manicured stub of a finger in my direction. "The last time a Pittsfield Murano was associated with organized crime was more than fifty years ago. Does old-school, name-ends-with-a-vowel organized crime still exist in Berkshire County? Yes, it does. But it's small-bore, piss-ant stuff — sports betting, a couple of numbers operations — and nothing that a type of person like Jim Sturdivant would need to be involved with or would ever be interested in getting anywhere near. The last mob homicide in this county was probably twenty-five years ago. Assault? That's another story. When the mob hurts someone, it's usually gambling-related, and the old-fashioned methods still apply. Knee-capping, leg-breaking, lead-pipe stuff. But shoot-to-kill is what the new guys do, the blacks and the South Americans, the serious drug operators. And unless Jim Sturdivant was Sheffield's heroin kingpin, his murder was not mob-related. Which leaves us with what, Mr. Strachey? Your client — angry, violent, unstable Barry Fields."

"Except," I said, "Fields didn't do it."

Cornwallis sneered. "You're so naïve."

"Fields had no weapon. He had no real motive. He's not dumb — after the cheese attack he had to know he'd be the prime suspect. He's volatile, but he's no fool."

"Fields has a history of violence. He can't control himself. He finally snapped and lost all control."

I said, "Fields is angry and argumentative. That doesn't mean a lot. Take you, for instance. You're angry and argumentative, but you don't go around shooting people. Some people, for a variety of reasons, turn out that way. They usually make poor spouses, and I wouldn't want one as my fifth-grade teacher. But if American society locked up all its deeply angry people, the country's incarceration rate would be even more ridiculous than it is now."

Cornwallis got even redder. Maybe he didn't appreciate my including him in the nation's prone-to-hissy-fit population.

As he glared at me and appeared about to let loose again, I added, "And then there's this additional complication. A lot of angry people have good reasons for being angry. Barry Fields certainly has one now. You've got him in jail based on next to nothing. And he may have other reasons too. What do you know about Fields' background?"

Looking dangerously scarlet now, Cornwallis spat out, "Get out."

"What do you mean?"

"Get. Out."

"You want me to leave?"

"That's what I said, yes. Just *get the fuck out of here.*"

He seemed to be struggling to hold back and prove me wrong after I called him a deeply angry man. But a major artery was throbbing on the side of the DA's neck, and I feared it might burst, spattering blood throughout the office if not the entire western side of Pittsfield's busy Park Square.

"Apparently I've made a poor first impression," I said. "I'm sorry. I actually thought I might be helpful. I still can be, I think."

"Just leave. *Now.*"

I said, "Barry Fields has a mysterious past. But I guess you know about that. That's one reason you're focused on him."

Cornwallis blinked. He said, "What do you know about Fields' past?" I could see his pulse rate drop marginally.

What I was thinking was, *Thorny, why don't you go first and tell me what* you *know?* What I said was, "Fields comes from a troubled background."

He didn't bite. "Yeah? Which is?"

"His parents died in a boating accident when Barry was six, and he was raised by porpoises in the Andaman Sea."

Cornwallis calmed down even further and said, "You don't know any more than I do about Fields' background, do you now, Mr. Strachey?"

"No, I do not. He is secretive about his past. His current identity goes back only about six years. Before that his life is a black hole."

"What we discovered," Cornwallis said, "is that Fields not only has no criminal record, he has no record of existing at all prior to his move to Great Barrington. Maybe in your mind, Mr. Strachey, that is a factor in his favor. In our minds it is the opposite."

I said, "What do you know about Jim Sturdivant's lending practices? His personal loans to acquaintances is what I'm referring to."

Cornwallis blanched, a trick for a man so florid. "I know more about the Sturdivant–Gaudios hot-tub loan office than I care to think about," he said. "The homosexual lifestyle is a mystery to me, and in my work I have become acquainted with practices that do not make it any less mysterious."

"And you don't think there's any connection between Sturdivant's financial practices and his murder?"

"Oh, but I certainly do see a connection," Cornwallis said, leaning toward me and looking smug. "Bill Moore was one of

Sturdivant's borrowers. Steven Gaudios is prepared to testify to that fact and to produce records. Obviously, Moore was having a sexual relationship with Sturdivant — one of the terms of the low-interest loan — and Fields had a jealous fit and attacked Sturdivant and then killed him." He sat looking at me coolly, as if my challenging this version of events would be foolhardy and stupid.

I said, "That's nuts. Moore climbed into the Sturdivant–Gaudios hot tub just once. It was before he and Fields were a pair. Fields heard about the transaction later, and he found it gross. But he did not expect Moore to be a virgin when they wed, and he was not sexually jealous. Fields was mad at Sturdivant because Sturdivant hired me to investigate Fields before he married Bill Moore. Sex had nothing to do with it."

Cornwallis almost smiled. He said, "What you apparently are not aware of, Mr. Strachey, is that Bill Moore happened to like getting into the Sturdivant–Gaudios hot tub. He did not visit it just once. He liked it, and he went back again and again. In fact, he visited the tub twice a week right up until the night of Jim Sturdivant's death, on nights when Fields was at work at the Triplex movie house. Steven Gaudios will testify to that fact also."

Gaudios. He was very deliberately framing Barry Fields, as if he knew who Sturdivant's killer was and was desperate to deflect attention. Why?

I said, "Gaudios is lying."

"I have no reason to believe so."

"He told you Bill Moore was in the hot tub on the night of the murder? Not so. Moore was working on a computer job in Springfield. I'm sure that can be checked out. Anyway, how would Gaudios know who was there that night? He was off playing bridge somewhere."

"Well, Gaudios didn't say Moore was there that night. But on recent nights he had been. That is *nights* plural."

I said, "You're being conned. You're so ready to believe that no man would ever turn down a blowjob when offered one — a conviction more commonly held by straight men than gays, I do believe — that you have been suckered into this horseshit story of Gaudios's. You apparently believe that all gay men ever think about is dick, when in point of hard fact many of us have a variety of other interests."

He peered at me confusedly. "You're gay too?" My impulse was to bat my eyelashes, but I just nodded. "I have no problem with gays," Cornwallis said.

"Peachy."

"I have a lesbian on my staff."

"You're so advanced."

"I'm not asking to be congratulated."

"I'm relieved."

"I happen not to agree with the church on homosexuality. We're all sinners, but this 'disordered' stuff is crap. I also know, however, that men do terrible things because of their sexual impulses. It's not a gay thing. It's a man thing. Gay men just happen to have more opportunities to fuck around and get in trouble and lose control of their emotions. The Sturdivant case is plainly one of those situations. It has crazed sexual jealousy written all over it. You're deluding yourself, Mr. Strachey, to believe otherwise."

Cornwallis was in love with a stereotype, and there was nothing I could do about it. To him this case was a simple queen-out-turned-violent, and he was stuck on that and not about to get unstuck. And it wasn't as though his version of events would have been unprecedented. The murderously jealous queen stereotype had some basis in fact. But it happened rarely — never in all my years of PI experience — and the theory was all wrong here.

I said, "I'm going to prove you're mistaken, Mr. Cornwallis. I'm going to ask you for some information about organized crime in Berkshire County and some names of people I can talk to about what's going on currently, mob-activity-wise. And you're going to give me that information just to watch me make a fool of myself. But then I'm going to surprise you and use this information and these contacts to find out who really killed Jim Sturdivant. And then you're going to thank me profusely and eat shit."

Cornwallis did not laugh uproariously at me, as I would have. He smirked. "Now there's an offer only a total dickhead could refuse. Sure, I'll point you in the direction of knowledgeable people. But if you lose a mouthful of teeth or get into a situation that ends up with organ failure, don't come whining to me."

Now he was relaxed and enjoying me. Cornwallis had hated me only minutes earlier, but now I was giving him huge pleasure. I couldn't wait to tell the guys back on Gordon Street that I had won over the fearsome Berkshire County district attorney.

Cornwallis consulted his computer while I waited and looked out the window. I watched a couple of three-car rollovers down on hectic Park Square, and some antiwar activists waving signs that read *Honk If You're for Peace*. The din was intermittent.

Soon Cornwallis wrote three names and phone numbers on a slip of paper and handed it across his desk to me.

He said, "You can say these referrals came from me, but I'm not sure how forthcoming any of these people will be." Then Cornwallis grinned — I didn't know he knew how — and said, "Don't hurt yourself now."

CHAPTER NINETEEN

Back in my car, parked on a side street near the Crowne Plaza Hotel, I phoned the numbers Cornwallis had given me. At one number, I got the voicemail of Johnny Montarsi and chose not to leave a message but to try him later. The second number was answered by the name Cornwallis had written down, Daniel Travio, but when I explained who I was and why I was calling, Travio told me to fuck off and hung up. Thorne Cornwallis's name was not yet working its magic.

Then I reached Tom O'Toole on his cell. Here was a last name with the vowel on the wrong end — had he changed it from Alioto? — which just went to show how thoroughly the forces of ethnic dilution and integration in America had done their job in recent decades. O'Toole said he was at that moment watching the Red Sox–Yankees game at an East Pittsfield bar, but the game was going badly and why didn't I drive over and distract him from the disaster?

G's Place was on Newell Street, near the now all-but-abandoned General Electric plant. The sports field across from the bar appeared shiny and new and looked like one of those let's-make-the-best-of-it civic projects where kids cavort above residues of toxic waste. The bar had the worn but durable feeling that's so appreciated in working-class neighborhoods where there isn't much work anymore. The place was nearly empty on this late summer Saturday afternoon, and I had no trouble locating O'Toole where he said he would be, on a barstool under the flat-screen TV, which as I came in showed a Sox batter chopping air.

"I'm Don Strachey."

"Tom O'Toole. Brew?"

"Sam Adams."

O'Toole sent an invisible message to the bartender, who produced a bottle and moved back down the bar.

"Thorne Cornwallis sent you over here? I haven't laid eyes on Thorny since he sent my brother-in-law Vincent to Cedar Junction four years ago."

"What's that, a camp for the performing arts?"

"Nuh uh. A penitentiary. Used to be called Walpole."

"Ah."

He must have weighed 300 pounds. He was in brown work pants whose contents spilled over the barstool like the great Boston molasses flood. His dark green T-shirt was fresh and clean and had the number *74* stenciled on the front. O'Toole was fiftyish, with soft, gray eyes and a flat nose. He smelled of cigarettes, aftershave and the Budweiser he was drinking. He had arms like stone Buddhas, and they made me contemplative, as they no doubt did others.

"Thorny could've put Vincent away for ten to fifteen, but he only asked for five," O'Toole said. "Mitzi appreciated that, and so did I. The gambling stuff, there was no getting around that. The assault with intent was not so clear-cut, though — everybody knew that flaming asshole had it coming — so Thorny let it go. I'm beholden to him because of it. And that, my friend, is why you **are** here." He looked at me with no particular expression.

I sipped my beer and then O'Toole sipped his. I said, "Jim Sturdivant. What do you know?"

"What do I know about what, Jim Sturdivant?"

"He was killed on Wednesday."

"Yeah. The guy was a pansy."

"You think that's why he was killed?"

"It's a good enough reason."

Could I just adroitly back out of this place? Yes, but then what? I said, "No, that's a poor reason. I disagree with you, Tom."

He shrugged, and something in the game caught his attention. He said, "Fuck."

I said, "It doesn't look so good for the Sox this year."

O'Toole looked back at me and said, "Jim Sturdivant was a pussy, that's what that fucker was."

"A pansy *and* a pussy. He was all over the place."

"The guy was older than me and I didn't know him, but I didn't like him," O'Toole said.

"How come?"

"How come what? What's to like?"

I said, "Cornwallis thinks a guy from Great Barrington shot Sturdivant, but I think he's wrong."

O'Toole eyed the Yanks' pitcher with disdain. He said, "Barry Fields. I don't know him. Works at the movie down there. He's a gay."

I said, "Cornwallis says the murder was about sexual jealousy. But Fields wasn't sexually jealous. Have you picked up anything about why Sturdivant might have been shot? If it wasn't sex-related, what else could it have been? Was Jim ever involved, for instance, in the kinds of activities his biological father was once involved in?"

O'Toole smirked. "You mean like sticking his dick in the hole nature intended? Nah, I never heard that about Jim."

"No, I mean loan-sharking or other organized crime activities."

He looked at me carefully now. "That was a long time ago. A lot of old people in Pittsfield remember Phil Murano."

"What I'm wondering, Tom, is if we have a case here of like father, like son. I know that Jim made a lot of money as a corporate flack. But maybe he had some other financial practices that weren't so well known. Not because he needed the money, but for sentimental reasons. Is that possible?"

Now O'Toole gave me the look he had just given the Yankee pitcher. "You mean like he was a chip off the ol' block? No. Jim Sturdivant was no Phil Murano in any way, shape or form. You got your head up your ass on that one."

"So you've never heard of Jim involved in any kind of what Thorne Cornwallis would consider illegal?"

He almost smiled. "Only butt-fucking."

"But, Tom," I said, "butt-fucking is legal now, too. There was a US Supreme Court decision several years ago. It helped pave the way, in fact, for the legalization of gay marriage in Massachusetts. Sturdivant and his boyfriend, Steven Gaudios, never married, however. Before he died, Jim told me family considerations prevented them from getting married. I guess the family would have objected."

"Objected!" O'Toole said, and grunted. "Jesus, Anne Marie would've fucking dropped dead! She's a frail old lady, and her son marrying a fag would've killed her on the spot."

All right, that was enough. "Tom," I said, "before we go any farther, I think I should tell you something about myself."

"Yeah, okay, just don't say you're queer too. If you did, this conversation would end right then and there."

So that's how it was going to be? Apparently. I said, "No, it's that I've been trying to place you since I walked in here. I think I remember you from college. Did you go to Rutgers, by chance?"

"Nah, Pittsfield High."

"It wasn't you then. There was a linebacker named O'Toole. I was an English major, but I always noticed the football players."

"Yeah."

What a dork. I said, "What about other members of Jim Sturdivant's family? Have any of them followed in Jim's father's footsteps?"

O'Toole puzzled over this. "Depends on what you mean by *footsteps*."

"Gambling, loan-sharking, assault, whatever."

After a moment, O'Toole said, "Well, there was Butch Murano."

"Who is he?"

"Jim's second or third cousin, he'd have to be. Butch ran a game for years in the back room at the Lakewood Grill."

"But not anymore?"

"That'd be hard. Butch passed on five or six years ago. Cancer of the tongue. It wasn't pretty."

"Any others? More recently?"

"Not any Muranos or Sturdivants that I can think of. Most of the stuff people used to deal in — your card games, your numbers, your horse betting, your whores — a lot of that's gone now. The Indians in Connecticut have ahold of the casinos. Hey, who says the white people won the war? The fucking Indians, they don't go to jail, plus they make out like bandits. You got your drugs, of course, but the blacks and the Mexicans control it all, basically. No Irish need apply. There's still lots of sports betting here in town, and it's still a nice, clean white people's way of doing business. It's seldom anybody gets hurt — not your blacks with their Uzis and their pit bulls chewing people's throats off. It's just roughing somebody up once in a while who bets and loses and neglects to meet their obligations. I've seen that happen."

I didn't ask O'Toole if he had seen that happen firsthand. I said, "What about Sturdivant's brother, Michael? He told a man who had him removed from a movie theater one time that the guy had better back off or he might get his leg broken."

O'Toole thought about this. "I've wondered about Michael."

"Wondered what?"

"People know him in Providence."

"Which means what?"

"Hey, you know Rhode Island."

"I guess you don't mean that in colonial times Rhode Island was a haven of religious tolerance."

"Nah, the mayor's in a federal prison. You don't get that in most places."

"Buddy Cianci. What was it? Rigged contracts? Kickbacks?"

"Yeah, nickel and dime stuff for a fucking mayor. What a putz."

"And Michael Sturdivant has friends of a certain kind in Providence?"

"I heard that. But what do I know?"

"Does Michael come to Pittsfield often?"

"I see him once in a while," O'Toole said and signalled the bartender for another Bud and another Sam Adams. "At mass at Mount Carmel with Anne Marie. He's a good son; you gotta give the guy credit. Unlike Jim. That fucker gave all his dough to the ballet and shit like that, and you seldom saw him in church. And he just lived down in Sheffield, unlike Providence two or three hours away."

"Michael must be in Pittsfield for the funeral. It's on Monday."

"Yeah, I saw him at mass yesterday. He was here earlier in the week too. I saw him over at Ern's Lounge on Fenn Street."

"Earlier in the week? Before Wednesday?"

"Monday, Tuesday. Dunno."

"Did you speak to him?"

"I said hi. What was I gonna say?"

"Who was Michael with when you saw him?"

"Anne Marie in church, and Rose, his sister. And in Ern's some guy, Cheap, from Schenectady."

"A man named Cheap?"

"They call him Cheap."

"What do you know about Cheap?"

"Nothin'. He's cheap, I guess."

"Maybe it's that he does bird imitations."

"Nah. He's too heavyset."

"What's Cheap's last name?"

"I think it's Maloney. Like baloney, but not."

"What does Cheap do?"

"Dipped if I know. He's just this guy you see once in a while."

"Who is Rose married to? Jim's sister."

"Some guy in Worcester, but they're divorced. She's a bitch, Mitzi says."

"Mitzi's your wife?"

"And the mother of my children."

"How many have you got, Tom?"

"Heather and Shaun. Shaun was a son of a bitch coming out, so Mitzi got her tubes tied. Father Ryan gave her some shit, and I had to talk to him, priest or no priest."

"Do Michael and Rose have children?"

"Maybe, but not around Pittsfield. They'd be in Providence and Worcester."

I said, "Except for Anne Marie, none of the Sturdivants stayed in Pittsfield. Why do you think that is?"

O'Toole shifted on his barstool, which creaked. "Lack of job opportunity. When power transformer went, Pittsfield went with it. We gotta get the GE back, is what this town's gotta do. But the mayor, those pricks. They don't do diddley. They're all in it for themselves."

"What do you do for a living, Tom?"

Now he chuckled. "I'm retired. What do you do, Don?"

"I'm a private investigator."

"Oh yeah. You said. Like Kojak."

"I think Kojak was a police detective, wasn't he? I've never been a cop."

"Keep it up," O'Toole said and raised his glass. "I have a niece who's on the police. She's a disgrace to the family. She's a dyke too. I don't know which is worse."

"Pittsfield sounds like a rough town to grow up gay in," I said.

"Gotta take pride in somethin', my friend."

From the car, I phoned a cop friend in Albany who had family and other connections in Schenectady. I asked him for information about a man known as Cheap Maloney, like baloney but not. He said he'd check. Then I tried Johnny Montarsi again, and this time he answered.

"I'm Don Strachey, a private investigator working on the Jim Sturdivant murder. Thorne Cornwallis said you might be willing to talk to me and give me some background information."

"What kind of information? I'm busy."

"Was Sturdivant involved in any kind of loan-sharking or other possibly illegal activities?"

"I wouldn't know. Thorny thinks I'd know about that, he's full of it."

"He didn't say that. He just thought you might have picked something up."

"Nah. I can't help. Anything else? I'm on my way somewhere."

I said, "Do you know Michael Sturdivant, Jim's brother?"

"Why? No."

"What about a guy named Cheap Maloney from Schenectady who comes to Pittsfield?"

Now I could hear Montarsi's breathing, even over our cell phones. He said, "Tell me your name again?"

"Don Strachey."

"Where do you work out of, Don? Springfield?"

"Albany."

"Uh huh. Hey, I wish I could help you out. Tell Thorny I wracked my brain. But this one I know nothing about. Honestly. Are you here in Pittsfield, Don?"

"Right now I am. I'm staying at a motel in Great Barrington, the Boxwood Inn. Maybe we could get together."

"Nuh uh, I'm tied up. Good luck with that Sturdivant thing."

"Thanks. Have a nice day, Johnny."

"You too, Don Strachey."

CHAPTER TWENTY

I picked Timmy up, and on the way back to Great Barrington I told him, "I want you to take a separate room at the motel. Somebody might be coming after me there."

"Coming after you? What's that supposed to mean?"

I explained that Johnny Montarsi, one of the well-informed local goons Thorne Cornwallis had referred me to, seemed to know who Michael Sturdivant and a dubious character from Schenectady named Cheap Maloney were, and Montarsi seemed inordinately interested in where I was staying and the fact that I was somehow connecting these two men to the Sturdivant killing.

"Jeez, Don!"

"And the thing is, this might be my most direct route to these two bozos. That is, baiting them."

"Baiting them to do what?"

"To show up. So I can talk to them. It's Cheap Maloney who'll have some insights to offer, I'm willing to bet."

"What if Cheap's most insightful expression comes by way of a lead pipe?"

"I can still handle situations like that. Are you suggesting that I'm over the hill, Timothy?"

"You? Oh, honey, never. Just because the AARP has your mailing address doesn't mean the Cosa Nostra does."

"This is not Cosa Nostra, not that big, I don't think. But I do believe Jim Sturdivant was involved in something that made some branch of organized crime want him eliminated. The hot-tub loans? No, I don't think it's connected to that. That was just some weird perversion Sturdivant enjoyed. Getting off by humiliating gay men because he was so ashamed of being gay himself. This is something else he did that got him killed, and there's circumstantial evidence that his brother, Michael — who may have mob connections in both Providence and Schenectady — is somehow involved."

"What evidence is there besides the fact that Michael was in the area earlier in the week before the murder?"

We were attempting to pass through the charming town of Stockbridge, with its Norman Rockwell Main Street and SUV gridlock. The rain had let up, and I could make out blue sky off to the west. As we sat stalled in the cloud of carbon monoxide that provided a cheap high for the tourists in rocking chairs on the front porch of the Red Lion Inn, I said, "Michael was here just before the murder. He's a wiseguy. The killing has the earmarks of a mob hit. This Montarsi mob guy seemed freaked that I was making the connection."

"Oh."

"Of course, what I'm saying here is, a man may have been involved in the murder of his own brother. I hate to think that."

Timmy said, "It does sound pretty biblical for Berkshire County."

"Not so Tanglewood-on-Parade, no."

"But Shakespeare and Company is just up the road in Lenox. That's a Berkshire institution, and there's plenty of fratricide in Shakespeare. In *Lear, Richard the Third, Macbeth*. And of course Claudius and Hamlet the father."

We edged forward another eight feet, and I said, "And Michael Corleone had Fredo shot."

"That isn't so Berkshires, except for the operatic score."

"I'm beginning to think the Sturdivants might be even worse in their own way than the Corleones," I said, as the car inched past the Red Lion and around the corner onto the road to Great Barrington. "Which would make sense. In my limited experience, real-life mob guys are much dumber and meaner than the Puzo-Coppola crowd, entertaining though they were. That's why mobsters love the Godfather movies. The films make them look tragic instead of like the worthless narcissistic twits they really are."

Timmy said, "What about Barry Fields' family, the ones he was so worried would show up? He insists they're not criminals, you said. Where do they fit in?"

"That I haven't figured out. Or the place in all this of Bill Moore, the assassin, who is in Washington supposedly being helpful in his very odd way."

"Or Bud Radziwill, the Kennedy cousin."

"I need to talk to Bud again. He knows too much about Fields to be getting off the hook so easily. This guy needs to be pressed a little."

"Pressed?"

"Persuaded."

"How would you do that? I mean, in a way that isn't hurtful."

"His friend Barry is a mental wreck. When I saw him in jail, Fields looked like he could be crushed for life by Thorne Cornwallis's idiocy. If Radziwill wants to help get Barry out of this, he has to tell me everything he knows. I'll appeal to his conscience. He especially has to tell me all he knows about Bill Moore — whose pal Jean Watrous, I found out, worked in the counterterrorism division of the FBI. Was Moore assigned there too? And if so, what does that mean, if anything?"

We were cruising south now on Route 7, the sun breaking through the clouds over Monument Mountain, its piney crags looming ahead of us. Timmy said, "I thought Moore was going to talk to you himself when he gets back from Washington."

"So he says." My cell phone twittered. "This is Strachey."

"I've got news about Mr. Maloney." It was my Albany cop friend.

"Is he bad?"

"Very. Horace Maloney, known as Cheap, did eight years in Dannemora on attempted murder, plus lots of mean, petty stuff as a youngster. My information is, Cheap is currently a mob enforcer and probably whackman. Cheap is an hombre to steer clear of, Donald, if that's your question."

"This is helpful. Thanks, pal."

"No trouble."

Timmy looked over at me warily and said, "Was that about Cheap Maloney?"

"It was."

"And is he a bad man?"

"You could say so."

"Are we still going back to the motel?"

"Yes and no."

Timmy said, "Let me think about that."

"Timothy, you're going to take your car and spend the night at home in Albany. Okay?"

"Okay."

"And I'm going to park my car with the New York tags registered in my name in front of our room. But I'm going to rent another car and spend the night in it at a spot in the motel parking lot with a good view of my car and the door to our room. I'll be armed and I'll be careful."

"How will you stay awake? You'll doze off."

"Coffee. Excedrin. I'll manage."

"Fear should help."

"That too."

"Is this guy Cheap really dangerous?"

"I'm told he is, yes. I'm going to call Joe Toomey, the State Police dick, and fill him in. Cornwallis is stuck on the wrong track, but Toomey may have an open mind."

"Yeah, and an arsenal bigger than yours."

I said, "Timmy, in all the years we've been together, this is the first time you've seen fit to denigrate my arsenal. I'm hurt."

"Better your feelings be hurt than your kneecaps, or your skull. Be careful, Don."

"That's my plan," I said, and truly believed at the time that I knew how to be.

Chapter Twenty-one

"Bud Radziwill has disappeared. I'm kind of worried about him. Has he been in touch with you at all?"

This was Ramona Furst, on my cell phone just as Timmy and I arrived back in our room at the Boxwood Motor Inn.

I said, "No, but I wanted to speak with Bud. What do you mean by disappeared?"

"Bud was at work at Barrington Video when a phone call came in from Barry at the House of Correction. Bud was agitated after the call and soon said he was going to have to leave. The manager was concerned and called me. He said Bud is always so steady and reliable, and he was afraid something was terribly wrong."

"Bud didn't say why he was leaving or where he was going?"

"No, and I've called his cell, and I even drove over to his apartment and knocked on the door. No answer — Josh must have left for work at Pearly Gates — and Bud's car is gone. I thought you might know something, Donald. I have a call in to Barry at the jail, but he's being interviewed by the jail shrink right now, and he can't call me back for another half hour."

"Why the interview? Are they worried about Barry's mental state? I know I am."

"The interview is routine evaluation and intake stuff. What do you mean, you're worried about his mental state?"

I told Furst about my jailhouse visit with Fields and his altercation over the TV channel and his general air of pessimism and despondency.

"Jail does that to people," Furst said. "You think they'll never bounce back, but most of the time they do, pretty much. Though it's true, after you've been through the deprivations and dehumanization of being locked up by the state in the company of sociopaths and other badly damaged people, you're never quite the same again."

I said, "I've seen a lot of people in jail, but Fields seems to me more wounded than most. We've got to get him out of there."

"Tell me about it."

"I know you're doing all you can, Ramona."

"That I am. One of the things I'm doing is depending on you. So what's your report, Donald?"

I described to Furst my lunch with David Murano and what I learned about Jim Sturdivant's criminal family background. I told her about my meeting with Cornwallis, and his casually — or maliciously — referring me to goons around Pittsfield likely to know about any current criminal activities by a Sturdivant, either Jim or his brother. Then I told her about Johnny Montarsi, and my mentioning to him that Cheap Maloney was seen with Michael Sturdivant earlier in the week, and then Montarsi's sudden sharp interest in who and where I was. I told Furst I had learned that Maloney was a man not to mess with, and I planned on approaching him gingerly.

"How about not approaching him at all?" Furst said. "Just turn your information over to Toomey and step aside. That's the only way to deal with those types, Don, believe me."

I said I wasn't sure there was time to let the wheels of justice turn at their usual glacial pace. I said it seemed to me terribly important that we get Barry Fields out of jail, and since I had helped put him there in the first place, it wouldn't hurt me to take a few risks. I was propped on a pillow on the motel-room bed, and I was aware of Timmy seated at the desk nearby, listening and frowning.

Furst said, "I'm calling Toomey myself to see if we can get his ass in gear. This sounds like valuable stuff you've come up with. Have you heard from Bill Moore? Where the hell is he in all this, anyway? Moore's being no help whatsoever. I don't get that."

"I've left messages," I said. "Moore is still incommunicado. I'd be prepared to believe he's onto the mob-hit angle and is using federal sources to help us out. But if he worked with his friend Jean Watrous at the FBI, he didn't work on organized crime. According to my bureau source, Watrous worked in counterterrorism."

"Really? Do you think Moore thinks Jim Sturdivant had some terrorist link? That's pretty far-fetched. We won't get far with Thorny on that one."

"Ramona, I haven't got a clue what Bill Moore thinks, or did, or is doing. But I know who probably does know. That's Jean Watrous. I'll try again talking to her. With Fields rotting in jail and Radziwill on the run, maybe she'll see how urgent all this is getting."

"Good luck with Jean," Furst said. "She's what I would call congenitally close-mouthed. Or maybe it's her training. Or some oath she swore on Dick Cheney's hunting license."

"I'll soon see."

I rang off and looked up Jean Watrous in the Berkshire County phone book. She was listed, with a Lee number, which I dialed.

"Yes, hello." She sounded out of breath.

"Hi, Jean. This is Don Strachey. I'm sorry we got off to a bad start the other day —"

"Don," she cut in, "I'm so sorry, but I can't talk to you right now. I have to go out of town unexpectedly."

"I'm calling about Barry — and Bud Radziwill. Bud apparently has disappeared —"

"Gotta go. I'm really sorry." Click, and she was gone.

"Oy vey."

Timmy said, "She hung up?"

"'Called out of town unexpectedly. Sorry, gotta run!' Timothy, why did these people hire me if none of them can bring themselves to trust me with the facts? If they just wanted to go through the motions, why not hire someone incompetent? Somebody who they knew would stumble around and, if serious trouble turned up, cut and run?"

"Some wussy defeatocrat."

"It's all too strange."

Timmy said, "Maybe they thought you *were* that incompetent person. If so, the joke's on them."

"Is it? I'm starting to wonder."

I phoned Joe Toomey on his cell and told him I was more convinced than ever that Jim Sturdivant was the victim of a mob hit, and I explained why I thought so. I told him about Sturdivant's father and brother and my conversations with Cornwallis, O'Toole and Montarsi. Toomey was amused that the DA had sent me chasing after men the state cop said were well-known Pittsfield thugs. But Toomey could not imagine why the mob would have it in for Jim Sturdivant — except for the ethically challenged but perfectly legal hot-tub loans, his record seemed spotless — and I had to admit that neither could I.

Toomey had not heard of Cheap Maloney but said he would do his own checking and meanwhile advised that I watch my back. I said I planned to. I told Toomey about Johnny Montarsi's interest in my whereabouts, and this made Toomey grow thoughtful. He said mob enforcers were not the kinds of people with whom I should reasonably expect to have a productive exchange of views, and I told him, yes, I had heard that.

Timmy and I picked up a rental car at a Subaru dealer near the motel, and I parked it in a shady spot across from my own car and the room I had rented. We had an early dinner at an excellent Japanese place on Railroad Street, and then Timmy headed back to Albany. I walked over to the Triplex, where the Saturday night throngs were converging. Myra Greene was in the lobby greeting fans, so I went in to say hello.

When she saw me, Greene looked apprehensive, even frightened. She cut off a conversation with a group of moviegoers and beckoned for me to follow her to a less crowded corner of the lobby behind a display of film noir memorabilia. A blown-up photo showed a blond Barbara Stanwyck with that seductive ankle bracelet marching down the stairs toward Fred MacMurray in *Double Indemnity*.

"Donald the gumshoe, oh, am I glad to see you!"

"I'm happy to see you got sprung, Myra. Thorny didn't hang you, but I guess he did rough you up a bit. I'm just glad you didn't have to blast your way out of the Great Barrington police lockup."

"Oh, I'm not worried about any of that, Donald. Cornwallis is just showboating — he's up for reelection in November — and that'll all blow over." Greene tried to gesture toward the "that," as if Cornwallis might be out in the parking lot surveilling the Triplex from his Berkshire DA's armor-plated Humvee, but her neck did something painful and she grimaced.

Then she said, "Barry's mother called him. I think this is gonna be trouble."

"In jail? She knew where he was — and who he says he is these days — and his real mother called Fields at the Berkshire County jail? I'm amazed."

Greene leaned my way, her old-time nicotine aura reaching up to me. "Barry called me a while ago. He called Bud first and told him to get out of town, and he said maybe I should take a little vacation too, because things were going to get ugly around here."

"Did he say who these problematical people were and how they were going to make their trouble?"

"Nuh uh. Listen, dear, now I'm just as curious as you are about who these pishers could possibly be." Greene waved to a couple of ticket-buyers she knew, and they waved back and each waggled a vigorous thumbs-up. It looked as if Thorny would not be collecting a lot of votes in Great Barrington come November.

I said, "What would you say was Barry's state of mind when he called? I saw him this afternoon, and he was despondent."

"Oh, he was angry when he called, Donald. Not gloomy, just fit to be tied. And kind of desperate to get out of the clink. That's why I'm telling you this, even though Barry said I should keep it under my hat. I'm worried about him, I have to tell you."

I said, "I'll alert Ramona Furst. She can call the jail psychologist, and they can keep an eye on Barry. He should have called Ramona himself, but I don't think he sees his family as a legal problem. He seems to regard them as something worse than that, a kind of moveable catastrophe, like war or global warming. Did he say he thought they might show up here in the Berkshires?"

"Donald, that's exactly what Barry's afraid of, that they'll come here and... do whatever it is they do."

"How did they locate him? Did he say?"

"On a gay-news Web site, he said. Barry's picture was on this Web site in a news report about him being accused of murdering Jim Sturdivant. His real name wasn't there, but he said his mother recognized his photograph."

"Barry's mother looks at gay Web sites? What's that supposed to mean?"

Greene screwed up her face, and I screwed up mine, and we just stood there.

In my car, en route back to the motel, I phoned Ramona Furst. I described my conversation with Myra Greene, and Furst said she would phone the jail and find out what she could. Furst said, "Why would Barry's mother be looking at gay-news Web sites? That's weird. Maybe despite being an arch homophobe, according to Barry, she was secretly proud of him, and she thought he might have become some kind of commendable gay personage, a young man of accomplishment. Is that possible?"

I said, "Not according to Barry, it isn't."

CHAPTER TWENTY-TWO

The night was warm for the Berkshires in September, and I sat with the rental-car windows open. The Boxwood Motor Inn was bordered by actual boxwood near where I had parked, and I was counting on its vaguely repellent perfume to help keep me awake as long as was necessary. The odd smell was actually an improvement over the new-car scent of the Subaru, which had eight thousand miles on it but must have been sprayed regularly with the stuff my Albany client used on his Washington Park rent boys. A complex engine is the human libido.

A vivid half-moon hung over the one-story motel, and bright, good-humored clouds moseyed by every so often. My view of my own car and motel room was clear, full and head-on. I had closed the drapes in the room and turned off all the lights. A nightlight burned above the door to my room, unit eight. A minivan was parked by the room to the left of mine, and just before midnight a car drove in and parked in the space to the right. A middle-aged man and woman let themselves into unit seven, and the lights stayed on until 12:40.

I had a big cup of good coffee with me, and it seemed that if I didn't really think about it much, a cigarette would have been nice. I had been off that ambrosial toxin for a long time, but on semitropical Nights in the Gardens of Great Barrington like this one, those old yearnings hung in the air mockingly. Of course, if I had actually smoked, I'd likely have projectile vomited the maki sushi I'd enjoyed several hours earlier across the parking lot onto the rear window of the shiny Lexus in front of unit seven.

I played the car radio quietly for a while, listening to the old jazz on WAMC. Some wonderful Coleman Hawkins numbers from the '40s gave me that wish-I'd-been-born-sooner feeling jazz from that era often does. Though if I'd been born sooner I'd be dead sooner and maybe already up in my mother's Presbyterian heaven, where all they played were Leroy Anderson favorites, a harrowing eternity of *Bugler's Holiday*.

At 2:21 a black Ford Explorer pulled in off Route 7. The Boxwood Motor Inn sign along the highway had its *no vacancy* section lit, but the SUV drove in anyway and paused in front of the motel office before slowly moving down the row of units that included mine. The vehicle came to a stop behind my Nissan. A figure stepped out of the front passenger side of the Explorer. He had what looked like a baseball bat in his right hand. The man was in work pants and a dark windbreaker and was tall and bulky.

I picked up my nine millimeter off the passenger seat beside me. The man with the bat did not pound on the door to my room or attempt to break it down. Instead, he smashed the windshield and headlights on my Nissan, did the same with the side and rear windows, and then got back into the SUV, which quickly rolled out onto the highway and turned north. I memorized the vehicle's New York state tags and then wrote the number down.

I thought, *Well, that wasn't so bad.* My pulse was pounding, but I was uninjured, I hadn't had to shoot anybody, or get shot, and my toothbrush and shampoo were safe inside the room. I hadn't learned much — just the license plate number of some vandals — but the incident certainly seemed to confirm that I had whomped a local Mafia hive with a stick, and all this mob mayhem had something to do with the murder of exemplary citizen and exquisite Sheffield homosexual Jim Sturdivant. That still made little sense to me, but finally I was getting somewhere.

Lights came on in several motel rooms, and the door opened to unit nine. A young man in sweat pants and a T-shirt looked out and around. The motel owner or night manager must have heard the commotion, and she came out wrapped in a sari. Both converged on my car and stood looking and exclaiming over the damage. I got out of the rental car and walked over.

I said, "That's my car. I guess we have to call the police."

They both stared at me.

"Weren't you in your room?" the motel lady said. "Why were you in that other car?"

"It's complicated," I said, and then I heard my cell phone ring in the rental car. I said, "Excuse me for one minute," and walked back to the Subaru.

"This is Strachey." I looked for the caller number, but it had been blocked.

A male voice said, "Your house on Crow Street gets it next, and then your boyfriend, Tim Callahan. Do you understand what we're saying?"

"Sure."

"Just leave it alone."

"Okay."

Click.

I went back to where four people now stood peering at my smashed car.

"I'll phone the police," the motel lady said and headed back toward the office.

The guy in the T-shirt said, "They only went after your car, not anybody else's. You must have pissed somebody off."

"I think I did."

"Any idea who?"

"Yeah, I think I know."

"Did you see it happen?"

"I did."

Now the guy just stared at me. Then he turned and walked back toward his room. He wanted no part of this, whatever it was. Smart. But he stood in the open doorway to his room to see what would happen next.

I had my phone with me now, and I called Timmy.

He answered immediately and said, "Don, wait. I've got someone on call-waiting. You have to hear this."

"Hear what?" But he was gone.

The motel lady came out of the office again and strode my way. She moved with more confidence now that she had called the cops.

Timmy came back on the line. "They got your office!" he said excitedly. "That was a night detective at Division Two calling. Somebody apparently firebombed your office, and a lot of the building is burning. Nobody seems to have been hurt, but your office is totaled. Don, I'm sorry, but are you okay?"

"Yeah, I am. How do they know it was arson? The wiring in that place dates to the Harding administration."

"Some of the crackheads in the parking lot saw it happen. Though the detective said he didn't have a good description of the bomb-thrower, and he wants to talk to you. Maybe you should come home if you're alert enough to drive. Did anything happen over there?"

I described my evening of excellent jazz and watching my car windows and headlights get obliterated. As I spoke, a Great Barrington police cruiser turned in off Route 7, its flashers putting on their light-show for no apparent reason.

Timmy said, "So there was no frank and useful exchange of views with the window-smasher?"

"No, I didn't even follow him. I ID'd the vehicle, so there didn't seem to be any point in trying to tail him. Or maybe I'm just more cautious than I used to be. Or in middle age I'm losing my nerve. What time was the firebombing?"

"Around one-fifteen, the police said."

"It could have been the same guys as here. There was time for them to drive over here. Actually, after they did a job on my car, they phoned me."

The Barrington cop was looking at the damage with a flashlight and talking with the motel lady, and they both glanced my way from time to time.

"What do you mean, they phoned you?" Timmy said.

"They had my cell number. They must have gotten it from Johnny Montarsi. They warned me off the case. Or that was my interpretation. They also mentioned your name, Timothy. They warned me off the Sturdivant case, and then they mentioned your name. If you get my drift."

"Oh. Well. Oh."

"They also said something about our house being next. So here's the deal. You have to visit your sister in Rochester. They won't know about Maureen. And I'll call some people to keep an eye on our house."

"Who?"

"Some people from South Pearl Street you'd rather not hear about. They'll do it for money."

The Great Barrington cop was coming my way now, followed by the motel lady.

Timmy said, "There's no way I'm going to Rochester. I'm coming over there."

"Mr. Strachey?" the officer said.

"Timmy, I have to speak with a policeman now. All right, don't go to Rochester. Drive over here, check into another motel, and then call me and tell me where you are."

He agreed to this, and I told the cop I needed to use the john and I would be right with him. In my motel bathroom, I placed a call to Albany and arranged for our Crow Street house to be protected in return for an exorbitant fee that was only a little less than Bill Moore was paying me. Oh, yes, Bill Moore, Bill Moore, Bill Moore. Where the hell *was* Mr. FBI agent / assassin / hot-tub borrower / same-sex bridegroom, anyway?

The police officer was young, well-scrubbed and looked at me suspiciously. He asked for my ID, which I produced, including my PI license. He said, "Do you have any idea who did this, sir?"

"I do," I said, and told the cop that I had been having an affair with the actress Pamela Anderson, who, I said, was currently appearing in a play at the Williamstown Theater Festival. I said I had heard that Ms. Anderson's manager believed it was her daily frequent bouts of incredible sex with me that were causing the actress to repeatedly blow her lines, and by smashing up my car the manager was warning me away from his distracted and exhausted client.

"What's this manager's name?" the cop said.

"Shel Glazer."

"He's in Williamstown?"

"I'm not sure where he's staying."

The officer's radio crackled, and he went over to the festively lit cruiser to deal with some more urgent matter. I took the opportunity to rapidly collect my belongings from unit eight. The cop was still yacking on his radio when I came out, so I took this additional opportunity to climb into the rental car and drive away.

CHAPTER TWENTY-THREE

So I was going to have to do this myself. To bring the cops in in a big way was to risk Timmy's safety, and mine, and our Albany home. The police and the DA would have to finish the job when the time was right. But for the moment I would have to be the one to shine a light into the chaotic and violent jungle to which Jim Sturdivant had somehow led so many of us. As I drove south into Great Barrington and thought about poor Barry Fields and his horrible family about to show up in the Berkshires, I began to see faint glimmerings of how I might sort all this out and keep all or most of the innocent parties from getting hurt. But that would take some luck and some arrangements.

I parked outside the Dunkin' Donuts just south of downtown Great Barrington and made some calls. It was after three a.m., and I was reluctant to waken Ramona Furst, but I did.

An immediately alert Ramona said, "I'm glad you called. I was going to call you, but I didn't want to waken you."

"Actually, I was up."

"I wasn't, but I was sleeping crappily, so it's just as well you called. The thing is, Barry is in Two Jones. That's the involuntary-admission psych unit at Berkshire Medical Center in Pittsfield. He's on a suicide watch. The jail psychologist isn't sure Barry isn't faking it. It could be a way of making sure his family can't get near him. Or it could be a genuine reaction to his hated family's arrival here. Supposedly, they are on their way from somewhere in the Midwest. Whatever Barry is feeling or doing, I'm worried as hell about him."

"That stinks. Poor Barry. So who *are* the awful Fields family, or whatever their names are? How did they identify themselves?"

"His mother wouldn't say. She just told the jail CO she spoke to that she and the rest of Barry's family — she said his real name was Benjamin — were coming to reclaim him, from the jaws of Satan or some crazy crap like that. And they would be here by Monday. She also asked about Jim Sturdivant's funeral, when and where it was."

"The funeral?"

"I'm wondering about that. If they're so awful, why would they want to pay their respects to the man their son is accused of murdering?"

Now it was coming clear. I got goose bumps, and I was hit by a sudden wave of dizziness. I said, "Did the officer tell them about the funeral? Not that it would be hard to find out about. It was in the paper. The funeral is Monday at ten at Mount Carmel Church in Pittsfield."

"I think he did tell them, yeah. Even though the mother did sound like a real piece of work, the CO said."

I wanted to do some checking to confirm my awful suspicions about Fields' family, so I told Furst my immediate concern was dealing with the thugs who had smashed my car, torched my office, and warned me off the case.

"The thugs who did *what?*"

I described my incident-filled evening, eliciting exclamations and gasps even from this woman who had seen far more of the criminal world than your average Berkshire professional woman had. I said, "I'm more certain than ever that Sturdivant was killed by a mob hit man, possibly this guy Cheap Maloney from Schenectady. The remaining big question is, why?"

"Another remaining big question," Furst said, "is how are you going to develop enough evidence to get Thorny to accept this inconvenient truth and go after the mobsters and release Barry?"

"I'm giving that a lot of attention," I said, "as is well-traveled Bill Moore, supposedly. Have you heard from Bill?"

"No, but I left a message on his voicemail about Barry being moved to the psych unit. Surely he'll call me."

"Yeah, surely." I told Furst I still had some other matters to attend to and I would be in touch later in the morning. She said she was going to try to get some sleep, and I said that sounded useful.

I called Division Two in Albany and talked to an officer about my bombed office. He assured me that no one had been injured, but he said my second-floor office was a charred wreck and the office of the divorce lawyer next door was also ruined. The vacant storefront below me had been badly damaged, as had the consignment shop next to it. The thought of my office being gone hurt a lot. All my computer files were backed up on discs at home, but my main workplace was an extension of my personality — frayed, sturdy, quirky, messy — and it felt as if a central piece of my life in Albany had been extinguished prematurely. There was also the matter of the signed photograph of jazz great Anita O'Day that had hung on the wall next to my desk, and for that loss someone was going to pay dearly.

The cop said a detective wanted to speak with me as soon as possible, and I obediently wrote down his name and number. Though for a number of reasons that would have to wait.

I phoned my Albany cop friend who had been helpful checking out Cheap Maloney. He didn't answer and was no doubt asleep, and I left a message giving the tag number and asking him to identify the owner of the Explorer that had carried the burly window-smasher to the Boxwood motel an hour and some minutes earlier. I asked my friend to let me know what he came up with as soon as he could.

Then I called AAA and asked them to tow my useless car to the Subaru garage where I had rented the car I was sitting in outside the donut shop. By then, the time-to-make-the-donuts aromas were wafting heavily through my window, though eating anything at all felt as if it would be asking for trouble — nausea, semiconsciousness, etc. — so I sat tight.

Timmy phoned soon after and told me he had taken a room at a Comfort Inn on Route 7, and why didn't I drive over and get comfortable? I was there in six minutes.

"This is getting dangerous," he said as I sprawled on the bed next to him. "This is not what you had in mind when Jim Sturdivant asked you to check up on a supposed young con man who was going to marry Sturdivant's dear, dear friend."

"No, Timothy, none of this is at all what I had in mind."

"And getting me onto some mob goon's hit list is not what you were after either. As far as I know."

"No, if I wanted you offed, I'd do it myself. I'd smother you with my love, and your muffled cries would haunt me for days."

Timmy said, "What do you think chain-motel bedspreads are made out of? Recycled Pepsi bottles? Where does that smell come from? If these bedspreads could talk, what would they say? Perhaps Jimmy Hoffa was killed by the Mafia, ground up, and stuffed deep inside a motel bedspread. Maybe *that's* the smell I'm trying to locate. Maybe the same thing will happen to you, and to me. And quite soon. Would you care to comment on my speculation?"

I said, "I'm on top of the mob angle. Yes, we both have to be careful. These are bad, violent people. You can still go to Rochester if you want to."

He said, "Nah."

"Steven Gaudios knows who these people are, I'm certain. I'm going to give him one more chance to tell us who killed Sturdivant and why. It's something the two of them were up to that drove Sturdivant's brother Michael completely over the edge. And I think he had Jim killed, and then he told Steven to get out of town or the same thing would happen to him."

Timmy was listening, but I could sense his breathing slowing down, and although he was still in his khakis and T-shirt, the idea of sleep was massaging his supple mind. I thought I knew, however, how I could sharpen his attention, if not make him sit bolt upright.

I said, "I still don't know what Sturdivant did to enrage the mob, but one thing has become clear. Barry Fields and his unhappy family situation had nothing to do with it. If anything, Barry's cheese-wheel attack on Jim in Guido's was a fortuitous coincidence for the killer, who saw it as a chance to get rid of Jim and frighten Steven without the police and DA looking beyond what to them was the obvious, and digging deeply into Sturdivant's and Gaudios's affairs."

Timmy murmured, "Right."

"The reason I'm so sure Barry's family had nothing to do with it is this: I'm reasonably certain I now know who they are."

His eyes had closed, but now they fluttered. "Oh really? Who are they?"

I told Timmy about Barry being taken to the psych unit in Pittsfield, where he was on a suicide watch.

"Oh no," he said and grew alert.

I told him about Barry's mother phoning him at the jail and informing him that the family was on their way to Pittsfield. I said Barry's mother also asked a corrections officer about the Sturdivant funeral, which was scheduled for Monday at ten.

I said, "What awful people have made it a practice to turn up at gay people's funerals all over the country?" Timmy was awake now. "What large extended family and their religious followers go to gay funerals and wave signs that say *God Hates Fags* and *Homos Will Burn in Hell?*"

Timmy said, "No."

"I think so."

"Barry is a — what? Grandson of Reverend Felson?"

"Barry's from the Midwest. Reverend Fred Felson operates out of a Baptist church in Topeka. Bud Radziwill told Ramona Furst that Barry and Bud met in the Emerald City, meaning Barry probably followed the Yellow Brick Road — as you yourself sagely speculated — out of whatever hellish situation he came from. That'd be Kansas. Barry told me he didn't think his family had anything to do with Jim Sturdivant's death because they don't have to kill people with weapons, that they have their own means for murder. That sounds like the Felson family, the people who picketed Matthew Shepherd's funeral and screamed that he had it coming."

Timmy was sitting up now. "And Reverend Felson is on his way to Pittsfield?"

"I think so."

"God, that makes it more urgent than ever that we get Barry out of jail and safely away from both Thorne Cornwallis and away from his family!"

I said, "I know."

CHAPTER TWENTY-FOUR

I set Timmy's alarm for eight and fell into a deep sleep that was interrupted by the alarm's bleat before I could get any terrifying dreams revved up. Timmy woke up apparently refreshed and headed for the sink and mirror. Raised Catholic, he observed a Muslim-like ritual of step-by-step ablutions involving several gallons of water, numerous potions, and a carton of appliances he carried with him whenever he left the house overnight. I had thought this might be a habit he'd picked up during his Peace Corps years in a predominantly Muslim section of India, but Timmy's sister Maureen once told me that he had always been what she called a "bathroom hog." I said something about it early in our relationship, and he replied, "You might try freshening up a little more extensively yourself once in a while." And that was it for that subject.

While Timmy abluted, I made some calls. I remembered from news stories that Reverend Felson's church in Topeka was the Southboro Baptist Church, so I retrieved the church's number from Verizon and dialed it. It was just after seven Sunday morning in Kansas, and a female voice answered the phone. When I asked to speak to Reverend Felson, I was told he was out of town for several days, and did I wish to speak to the assistant pastor? I said no and asked if the reverend was headed for Massachusetts. "Yes, the pastor is descending into the belly of the beast, and we must all pray for him," the lady said. I told her I was actually calling from Satan's lower intestine and wished her a good day.

I called Ramona Furst, who said, "Bill Moore will be back in town later this morning, and he wants to see you."

"Finally. So what's Bill's report?"

"He just said he'd talk to you and will phone you when he gets to Great Barrington. He sounded upset, and he's very concerned about Barry. I'm going to try to get him into Two Jones to see Barry this afternoon."

"He didn't say what he came up with in Washington? Supposedly Moore was going to gather information that was so crucial that it was okay for him to disappear for over forty-eight hours. That's what he told Bud Radziwill."

"No, he sounded totally frustrated with whatever he ran into down in DC."

I said, "Maybe the guy is some kind of pariah at the FBI, or wherever it was he worked. Maybe there was something he did that was especially controversial or politically embarrassing to the Bushes, and nobody dares speak with him."

"Or maybe," Furst said, "whatever Bill dug up is not exculpatory for Barry. That, we don't need."

I told her what I had deduced about Barry's horrendous family, the Felsons.

Furst said, "Dear God."

"Exactly."

"And you think it's Reverend Felson who's on his way here to reclaim Barry?"

"I do."

"We have to save him!"

"We will. One way or another. I have some preliminary thoughts about that."

"Are you safe yourself? From the thugs?"

"I'm okay," I said, "as long as they think I'm off the case. Has Radziwill turned up? Or Jean Watrous? They must have heard from Barry that Reverend Felson is headed this way, and that's why they ran for their lives."

"I've had no word from either of them. Don, if Barry is really a Felson, I wonder what Bud is?"

"Think Texas," I said. "That's his accent, no?"

"Actually," Furst said, "Bud sounds more like a guy I know in Pittsfield, a painter from the Southwest, who talks the same way. But there are differences between his and a Texas accent. Bud's is softer and sweeter than Texas, with its *y'alls* all the time. I'd say Bud — no Kennedy cousin, for sure — is not so much Texas as Oklahoma."

I went quickly through my News of the Week brain Google, and that's when something else clicked. I said, "I'll ask

Bud if he's from Oklahoma when I see him, as soon as this is all over. Which is going to be quite soon."

"For Barry's sake, and yours, and Timmy's, it had better be over soon."

"Noted."

I reached Joe Toomey's voicemail and gave him a crisp summary of recent events. I was planning on asking for his help soon, and it was important that he be kept up to date. I considered trying to reach Thorne Cornwallis. But he plainly was a man who would have to be handed the truth on a silver platter — and then maybe have his face shoved in it — and that was impossible until I knew why the mob had so badly wanted Jim Sturdivant dead.

After I showered, Timmy and I availed ourselves of the "continental" breakfast in the motel lobby — the "continent" must have been Trans-Fatia — and picked up the Sunday papers at a nearby convenience store. The *Berkshire Eagle* again led with the Sturdivant murder. The story had no new actual information, though that was not a hindrance to the paper's covering much of its front page with photos of smiling Jim Sturdivant and glowering Thorne Cornwallis and a wordy recap of the bloody crime.

Timmy chose to stay at the hotel and make his way through the Sunday *Times* while I visited Steven Gaudios. During the drive down to Sheffield, I tried Bill Moore's cell phone again, and this time he answered.

"Let's have lunch," Moore said. "Didn't Ramona tell you I was on my way back?"

"She did. So are you going to show up for lunch this time, or will you do your vanishing act again? I've had enough of that."

"No, you can depend on me this time, Strachey. I mean, up to a point. The thing is, I didn't find out what I thought I would find out, I'm sorry to say."

"Stuff happens, to quote our secretary of defense. But what did you learn?"

"Listen, I'm down on Route 7 in Connecticut, and the cell service is spotty. Let's meet at my house at twelve. We can order pizza."

I thought, *Here we go.* "You bet, Bill. See you at noon at your place." And don't assassinate anybody in Falls Village as you pass through. Pizza for lunch? On four hours' sleep, I'd be dozing by mid-afternoon. I was feeling crankier and crankier, and I had my reasons.

Down in Sheffield, the Gaudios–Sturdivant house was quiet. One of the BMWs was gone, but the convertible was in the driveway with its top down. The *For Sale* sign was still in the yard. I parked behind the Beemer and walked around back. The pool was deserted, as was the hot tub, and the rhubarb that marked the grave of the martini-drinking terrier.

I went up the back steps and banged on the screen door. Gaudios soon appeared, in Bermuda shorts and a fresh white polo shirt, and he looked annoyed, so very, very annoyed, to see me.

"You just don't know when to quit, do you, Donald?"

"Did you think I was off the case, Steven? Is that it?"

"I can't invite you in. I am incredibly busy."

I tried to open the screen door, but it had been latched from inside. I drove my fist through the screen and unlatched the door. Gaudios fell back and went for a cell phone on the kitchen counter. I grabbed it from him and snapped, "Sit down."

"You don't know who you're dealing with," he said bitterly and flopped onto a kitchen chair.

"I'm dealing with the mob," I said. "And you're one of them."

"Ha!" Gaudios snorted, and threw his head back like Tallulah.

"You and Jim were into something the mob didn't like. The mob, in this case, being, among others, Jim's brother, Michael, a wiseguy in Providence."

Gaudios's face contorted, and he looked away.

I said, "The hot-tub loans, they were nothing. Just a couple of obnoxious rich queens playing games with younger gay men who were poorer in wealth but often richer in spirit and integrity."

"What a horrid thing to say!"

"But you two had some other racket going, with much higher stakes, that helped get you your houses in New York and Palm Springs and Ibiza and all the rest of it. Along the way, however, you were stupid and reckless enough to cross somebody — somebody treacherous and big and mean. And whoever it was that you fucked with had Jim killed and then ordered you to get lost before you were whacked, too. Am I right?"

Gaudios was slowly shaking his head as tears streamed down his face. "You're wrong, Donald. You are so, so wrong!"

"Are you telling me that the goons who smashed up my car last night and threatened me and Timmy if I kept trying to clear Barry Fields were not mob guys connected to Michael Sturdivant? Don't tell me that, Steven, because the evidence is mounting. And where I am treading, Thorne Cornwallis will follow close behind. You can partially redeem yourself by cooperating, and I'm sure you can get into the Witness Protection Program and still live like a prince on some tropical isle where you can resume your hot-tub operations and enjoy a long life of strong martinis and copious dick. But now, finally, you have to tell the truth."

Gaudios sat transfixed by my monologue. Then he said quietly, "Jim and I both made our money honestly."

"I don't believe you."

"I can show you."

"You're lying. All the evidence — everything I know and have seen in the past three days — says you're lying."

"Come with me." He got up, and I followed him closely through the dining room and into a small study.

I said, "If you've got a gun in here, forget it." I produced my nine-millimeter and aimed it at him.

"You're awfully melodramatic, Donald. I thought private eyes only waved revolvers around in cheesy TV shows."

"Dealing with you represents a special occasion," I explained.

Gaudios sat behind a beautiful mahogany desk with a tidy surface and retrieved some Smith Barney statements from a drawer. He spread them out for me to look at. I perused the documents and saw that Gaudios's assets were diversified and his net worth, just from the accounts in front of me, totaled maybe thirty-five million dollars.

I said, "Money-laundering works wonders. Congratulations."

He said, "I worked in financial-institution mergers and acquisitions for thirty years. My fees and commissions were generous. I was also both prescient and lucky. Note my one hundred Berkshire Hathaway shares. I purchased those shares in 1978 for a hundred and sixty dollars each. Today they are worth a hundred and eight thousand dollars each."

I had watched CNBC for an hour once, and all of this sounded plausible. This was how capitalism worked for the people who had thought it up and had found ways to stay awake through *Wall Street Week*.

I said, "You called in the hot-tub loans, and when one of the borrowers protested, you threatened to break his legs. Did you pick that particular technique up in mergers and acquisitions?"

"Oh, that was just my anti-depressants talking. I could no more break anybody's legs than spit nickels. Really, Donald, just how butch do you think I am?"

I said, "But gangsters killed Jim. Of that I am certain. Why?"

Gaudios looked me hard in the eye and said, "No, Barry Fields killed Jim. And you have been conned by a very disturbed but very clever young man."

"No, Steven. Barry Fields is no killer. He is an angry young man with plenty to be angry about. And you'll soon see up close why he is so terribly angry. But murderously violent he is not."

"Really? How can you be so sure?"

I said, "Was Jim's biological father a Mafioso?"

Gaudios was unperturbed. "He was. It was a terrible embarrassment for Jim, growing up in Pittsfield with people knowing his father had died in a jail-yard stabbing."

"And Jim's brother, Michael? Has he not carried on a fine family tradition?"

Gaudios was sweating lightly now, even in this exquisitely furnished room cooled by all-but-noiseless central air-conditioning. He said, "Jim had his suspicions, but he never really knew much about Michael's life in Rhode Island. I think it's fair to say Jim didn't really want to know. Jim and I built a life far, far away from certain unhappy elements of our childhoods — criminality, yes, but not just criminality. The life we made together would have been even farther away had Jim been willing to live apart from his mother. But he was devoted to Anne Marie, and so here we are — or were — a stone's throw from Pittsfield and all that old pain. It hasn't been easy, in that respect. But I must say, in our own way, we've had our deep satisfactions. And our revenge."

"Revenge?"

"Living well is the best revenge, as Abraham Lincoln said."

"And so," I asked Gaudios, "who, then, are these mob goons who have threatened to hurt me and Timmy if I don't get off the case and quit trying to free Barry Fields?"

Gaudios was all serene now. "I really couldn't begin to answer that question, Donald. Perhaps it's something you stirred up or got into up in big, bad Pittsfield. It certainly has nothing to do with Sheffield, or with Jim's death, or with me."

He sat looking at me levelly, no longer frightened and teary.

I knew he was lying, but I didn't know how or why. I told Gaudios I would be back, and I got up and went out. As I walked down the back porch steps, I thought I heard him sob once.

CHAPTER TWENTY-FIVE

I drove back to the motel and told Timmy about my meeting with Gaudios.

He said, "So if Steven is lying and he's in touch with the mob guys, won't he alert them that you're still working on the case and you haven't been frightened off?"

"This is possible."

"All the more reason to wrap this one up fast."

"Yes, I would say so."

I told Timmy I was having lunch with slippery Bill Moore, and he said in that case he would accept Preston Morley's invitation for a hike up Monument Mountain and a picnic there with Morley and David Murano. Timmy said this was the spot where Hawthorne and Melville once picnicked together and set off intellectual sparks that may have set the course of American literature for the next fifty years.

I said, "I'm sorry I can't come too, but I've got a more immediate and up-to-the-minute bundle of sparks to set off."

"I wouldn't dismiss the relevance of Hawthorne and Melville to this case," Timmy said. "Hawthorne was haunted by his family's past in Salem, and Melville by what he had seen and done as a young man at sea. The Sturdivant murder seems to have a lot to do with the past catching up with people who thought they had outrun it."

"Or who thought they could both escape the past and exploit it at the same time."

We sat there, the Sunday papers spread out around us on the motel bed with the bedspread you didn't want to get too close to. Did we know what we were talking about? As it happened, yes and no.

Moore's Honda was parked in his driveway. I pulled in behind it and went up the front steps of his pleasant house on its pleasant hillside. Despite the strain he was under, Moore looked fresh and fit in clean jeans and a navy blue T-shirt. I followed him into the living room with the giant TV and the movie memorabilia. He offered me a beer, and when I declined, he said, "I guess I better stay sober myself. I'm seeing Barry at three, and he won't appreciate it if I'm fucked up."

"How is Barry doing? What have you heard?" I seated myself on one of the leather chairs. There was no sign of pizza — a relief — just some bar nuts in a dish.

"He's okay, Ramona says, and they've got some good shrinks keeping an eye on him. But Barry really needs to get away from here as soon as he can. He is not a violent person, but I'm really afraid of what he'll do if his family actually shows up here. What a fucking nightmare."

"I know who they are," I said.

"Yeah, Ramona told me you figured it out."

"I understand why he doesn't want to have anything to do with them, and why he would not want it known that he was a relative. What's the relationship? Is Barry Reverend Felson's grandson?"

Moore nodded. "Barry's mom, Edna, is Fred's third daughter. His dad is Warren Krider, one of Fred's loony flock. Barry's real name is Benjamin Krider. Warren and Edna tossed him out on the street when he was seventeen after they caught him in bed with a kid in his Bible study class. They didn't even try to have him de-programmed or exorcised. The nutty de-gaying approach is for the relatively more enlightened Evangelicals. The Kriders just told Barry he was an agent of Satan and to get the hell out."

"That he is bright and decent didn't figure in, it looks like."

"No, bright and decent are not what Christianity is about with the Felsons. Dumb and hateful is the rule. How Barry survived his own family with nothing worse than a lot of anger is a mystery. He can't explain it himself. He thinks he may have learned how to be human from a couple of teachers he had in school, and from old movies he rented and watched when Edna and Warren were out protesting against homosexuals. Some parents have to worry that their kids are home watching porn, but Barry once told me he was led astray from his family by watching M-G-M musicals, Frank Capra and Truffaut."

"The Reformed Church of Arthur Freed. I'd have signed up for that. So Barry left Topeka when he was seventeen?"

"He hitched a ride to Denver, the gay mecca of the mountains and plains. He knew about Denver because the Felsons had picketed AIDS-victim funerals there, and Barry had gone along a few times and seen all the counter-protesters. So he knew right where to go. He shacked up with a guy he met in a park for a while, and then he met Bud Radziwill at a gay community center. Bud's family hadn't thrown him out, but they were so homophobic that he ran away on his own."

I said, "Bud Radziwill is really Bud Huffler, right?"

Moore looked startled. "How did you know?"

"He's from Oklahoma, I've been informed by an expert amateur linguist. I knew his story was similar to Barry's because Bud told me his family were homophobic horrors, too. The most infamous public homophobe in Oklahoma is Republican Senator Elwin Huffler. He's the man who, during a debate on the anti-gay-marriage constitutional amendment, stood on the Senate floor and bragged that no one in his family had ever been divorced or had ever been a homosexual."

Moore said, "Yeah, that's Bud's granddad. A piece of work."

"Isn't Bud ever tempted to make a liar out of that awful clown?"

"I don't think so," Moore said. "Bud just wants a life. Like the rest of us."

"So he and Barry met in Denver and became pals?"

"They were boyfriends for a week or so, but the chemistry just wasn't there for that and they decided to be friends instead. They got restaurant jobs, and when they got worried about Bud being tracked down by his family, both of them decided to change their identities and make a complete break from their old lives. Some of the illegal Mexicans they met in the restaurant where they worked showed them how to get fake IDs."

I said, "It's ironic that Congress — including Senator Huffler — is beside itself over all the aliens with phony papers, when remaking oneself has always been the quintessentially

American act. It almost ought to be a requirement of citizenship."

"Yeah, well."

"Oh, sorry, Bill. You must have to take the FBI's line on illegal immigration, you being a former agent and all."

Moore did not take this opportunity to enlighten me on his Washington career, and I let it go for the moment.

Moore smiled weakly and said, "Don't worry. I'm not going to turn them in."

"You're a regular fellow."

"Barry and Bud were very fortunate in Denver," Moore went on. "Somebody in the gay movement there put them in touch with the Hemmings Foundation, which arranges for college scholarships for smart, gay kids who are alienated from their families. So they both went to the University of Colorado, where they really thrived. Bud calls Boulder the Emerald City."

"It must have seemed magical after...where? Oklahoma City? Tulsa?"

"Enid. Not so cosmopolitan as Tulsa."

"And after college they came to the Berkshires?"

"They met some people in Boulder who'd gone to Simon's Rock College in Great Barrington, and this area sounded to them like a place that was both civilized for gay people and a long way from their families. So they just drove their old truck here after graduation, and you know the rest."

"That's an amazing tale, Bill. I admire those two brave guys immensely, and I'm going to do everything I can, within my meager powers, to make sure their good life in the Berkshires can continue. But first I'd like to hear the story of how and why you moved up here."

Moore scowled and shook his head. "No."

"Why not?"

"I hired you, Strachey, so that I would *not* have to demonstrate skills and knowledge I gained at the bureau, and so local people would not start looking at me in a certain way. I want my privacy, and I want my identity as a computer technician, and that's not asking a lot. And I'm not sorry I hired you to be me. You're good at it. A hell of a lot better than I was." He looked at me grimly.

I said, "You got drunk one night at Twenty Railroad and told a fellow drinker you had killed people during your career, and you were tortured by the memory of this."

His mouth opened and he looked around the room, as if to check if anyone else might be overhearing our conversation. Then he stared at me hard. After a long, tense moment, Moore said, "My real name is Willis Garwinski."

"That doesn't ring a bell for me. Should it?"

"Two people in Great Barrington know the truth about me — Barry and Jean Watrous. Jean and I were colleagues at the bureau."

"Oh, so you worked in counterterrorism. I know Jean did."

"You just know fucking everything about everybody, don't you, Strachey? Well, you'll be the third person up here to know about me, and you have to keep your goddamn mouth shut. Do you understand me? Can I trust you?" His face was flushed, and now he looked not so much frightened and angry as imploring.

I said, "I won't be aiding a felon, will I? I don't want Thorny throwing me in the lockup like Myra Greene."

Moore looked at me and said, "I am not a felon. I was never tried and convicted. Nobody was."

"Tried and convicted for what? We're you some kind of assassin?"

"Yeah," Moore said and clasped his hands together tightly as he seemed to shrink into his chair. "I was an assassin, all right. I killed three thousand people."

It was the number. My breath caught. I knew immediately what he meant. We sat looking at each other.

I said, "It was the system, the cultures, the bad leadership. You were not responsible."

He shook his head.

I said, "The FBI was there to prosecute crimes, and the CIA was there to gather intelligence, and the dolts in charge never cracked heads and demanded that the cultures merge and transform themselves to accommodate the new reality of international terrorism. No single person let nine-eleven happen, except maybe Clinton or Bush."

Moore said evenly, "No, mistakes were made by individual people, and I was one of them. It could have been prevented. It should have been prevented. There were people in the bureau screaming for clues to be taken seriously. There was the supervisor in Phoenix who asked headquarters to check out Arabs with suspicious backgrounds matriculating at US flight schools. There was the Minneapolis agent who reported Zacarias Moussaoui's weird interest in flying but not landing airliners, and then Washington declining a request to go into Moussaoui's laptop because there was no probable cause. Then there were the CIA dickheads who knew that al-Qaeda operatives involved in the bombing of the USS Cole were inside the US and refused to modify their procedures and hand over the names of these characters to some of our guys who were actually hot on the trail of something big — something big which they didn't know what it was until the day it happened."

I said, "I've read about some of this. Some FBI people were suspicious, and they were thwarted."

Moore said, "Well, take a good look at the man you're sitting in this room with. I was one of the thwarters."

"Jesus, Bill."

"Checking out every Arab in a US flight school would have tied up hundreds of agents for months, or years."

"And you didn't have the resources?"

"Counterterrorism was way understaffed and underfunded. And the way up in the bureau was always to put crooks in jail — crooks who had already committed crimes. That's what the bureau had always been for. Though basically the problem for me was, I was one of the people who thought, it can't happen here. God will protect the United States of America."

"Bill," I said, "or Willis. You're being way too hard on yourself. I'll bet other people have said, yeah, we were wrong, but now let's move ahead and get it right. That's the important thing, getting it right the next time."

"The other thing is, Strachey, I actually thought about taking some of this shit that was coming in more seriously and pushing harder. But I didn't do that, because in my career at the bureau I was never a boat rocker. I was always Mister Go-along, Get-along. I didn't dare be a troublemaker. I couldn't afford to draw too much attention to myself. And I think you know why."

"Oh. That again."

"It's ironic," Moore said, "in an organization whose headquarters is named for that candy-ass closet case J. Edgar Hoover. But the FBI is not an institution where out gay people can expect to move up. Or expect to be taken seriously at all."

I said, "But you must have been taken seriously enough — even though you're out of the closet now — that you thought you could go down to DC on Friday and knowledgeable people there would be helpful with the Sturdivant murder investigation. Am I right?"

"Yeah, there are people who still talk to me, in the bureau and at Justice. And they did help me out. I can confirm to you that Michael Sturdivant is involved in sports betting and numbers in Providence. And while he's never been convicted, Michael has probably badly injured a number of citizens in the course of his business activities. Michael is a baddie, for sure."

"This is helpful. It confirms what I picked up in Pittsfield."

"Our problem," Moore said, "is that there's nada on Jim Sturdivant and Steven Gaudios. I was pretty sure they were into something dirty, and that's why Jim got whacked."

"I thought so, too."

"It turns out, however, that they are model citizens. They got rich the way most people get rich in the US of A — legally investing in the honest labor of others."

"Which leaves us," I said, "with no plausible motive for Jim being killed by the mob. Except, the evidence is piling up that that is exactly what happened." I described to Moore my meeting with Thorne Cornwallis, my conversations with two Pittsfield hometown thugs, the apparent involvement with Michael Sturdivant of a Schenectady hit man, and the firebombing of my office and the attack on my car to warn me off the Sturdivant murder case.

Moore said, "Then they sure as hell did it. Those fuckers killed Jim. Christ, but why?"

"Maybe it was personal? Except, why would either of them have anything to do with these mob guys? Michael and Jim were brothers, and both of them seemed devoted to their mother, the sainted Anne Marie. But that seems to be their only current point of connection."

"Maybe," Moore said, "Jim did something to hurt Anne Marie and it set Michael off."

"Like what? Jim basically indulged her every wish and need, I've been told by Pittsfield people, including staying basically closeted north of Stockbridge so she would not have to face the ignominy of having begotten a fag son. And he left her a million-five. How could he possibly have offended her at this late date?"

Moore said, "What's a woman in her mid-eighties or older going to do with a million and a half dollars? That's a lot of bingo cards."

I pondered this. "So who is in *her* will? Is that what you're saying? Like maybe Michael is her heir, and she's in ill health, and if she died before Jim, the one-point-five would go to someone else, like Gaudios or the opera? But the way it works now, the money goes to Anne Marie and then, when she croaks, to Michael?"

"Maybe. Mob guys think that way. Even when family members are involved. Maybe *especially* when family members are involved."

"So," I said, "what we have to find out is, how healthy is Anne Marie, and who is in her will?"

Moore thought about this and said, "What else have we got?"

I thought about it too, and it just didn't feel like the answer. It was too tidy, too small, too shabby. Not that people's lives weren't sometimes snuffed out by smallness and shabbiness. The horror of that ugly truth — that the Clutter family could be massacred by a couple of dim punks, that JFK could be deleted from the American landscape by a bitter and confused creep who got off a series of lucky shots — was why so many people chose instead to believe in fate, or divine retribution, or vast conspiracies that don't exist. That people's lives could be ended for dumb, trivial reasons was just too awful for some people to contemplate, even though it was all too grotesquely true.

And yet, I still felt this wasn't about money. Jim Sturdivant's life had been too complex, too fraught, and his killing too seemingly out of the blue.

I said, "Bill, I'm sorry I called you an assassin. I wish you had told me the truth. I'd have been understanding, as most people would be."

He shrugged weakly. "I just don't want to be the man that people look at and say 'that's the man who...you-know-what.' I don't want to be that guy to anybody except myself. Which is hard enough, believe me."

"I understand now why both you and Barry first bonded over your carrying secrets that haunted both of you. But Barry's secret might soon be revealed, and I can't help suspecting that he'll be stronger and healthier for it. He won't be carrying the load nearly all alone. And maybe that could also be the case for you."

"Barry has been my savior, that's for sure," Moore said, his voice unsteady now. "He's been the one person who's been able to drag me kicking and screaming out of myself. And I didn't move to Massachusetts for its gay politics. I came here because Jean has been a real pal to me. But now that I am free and out of the closet, I just feel so goddamned lucky I live in a state where two men who love each other and are devoted to each other can stand up in front of their families and friends and the whole fucking town and proclaim their love and commitment, and then get recognition from the state for doing it."

"It's a truly wonderful thing," I said.

"I feel bad for people in other states who can't do it," Moore went on, "and also for people right here in Massachusetts who for religious or family reasons can't just go down to town hall and get hitched, even though they know in their hearts that their relationships are as deep and good and true as anybody else's."

I thought of Preston and David and how fortunate they were — maybe Timmy and I would have the chance to do this one day also — and I remembered at lunch on Saturday noticing Preston and David's twin silver wedding bands. Then I remembered someone else I had just been with who was wearing a silver band on his ring finger, and that's when it all came together.

CHAPTER TWENTY-SIX

On the way back down to Sheffield, I phoned Ramona Furst. She said Massachusetts state offices wouldn't be open until Monday morning, but it would be no trouble retrieving the information I was looking for. Meanwhile, she said, she was joining Bill Moore on his visit with Barry Fields, aka Benjamin Krider, at Berkshire Medical Center. I asked her to set up a meeting later that afternoon with Joe Toomey, and she said she would try. I told her it was crucial that we coordinate our plans for solving the Sturdivant murder case, for Toomey had the wherewithal and I had the facts.

Steven Gaudios was in the driver's seat of his convertible, his back-up lights on, about to head off somewhere. I pulled in behind him, the rental car's front bumper touching the BMW's rear. I got out, and he said, "Please move. I am expected for lunch, and I am already quite late."

"I haven't had lunch myself, Steven, but that'll have to wait."

"No, in my case lunch will *not* have to wait. Now please move your car! We have had our discussion, Donald, and there is nothing more for you and I to say to one another."

I said, "His family killed Jim because he got married to a man. That man would be you."

Gaudios gagged, and I was afraid he would retch on his car's leather upholstery or on his beautiful white shirt.

"Somebody in or close to Jim's family," I said, "discovered that you two were married and told Michael. He was afraid Jim's mother would find out, and the news would break her heart and embarrass her with the ladies at bingo and with the priests at Mount Carmel and with other family and friends around Pittsfield. So Michael hired a Schenectady enforcer named Cheap Maloney to kill Jim, ending the ungodly and embarrassing same-sex marriage and punishing both of you for your gross insult to diocese and mob ethics."

Gaudios was staring up at me wild-eyed and still coughing up a storm.

I said, "Then they told you to get the hell out of Berkshire County before they did to you what they did to Jim. And they no doubt told you that if word of the marriage ever came to light, you were finished."

Gaudios suddenly opened his car door and bolted toward the back of the house, still sputtering. I followed him as he zigzagged past the back porch, around the pool, and over to the hot tub, where he vomited into the still waters.

I stood aside as Gaudios retched copiously, gagged dryly a few times, and then fell back gasping against a chaise lounge. He noticed that his pretty shirt was spattered, and he pulled out a handkerchief to wipe away some of the mess.

I said, "I would be far more sympathetic, Steven, if you hadn't been so eager to let Barry Fields take the rap. What a despicable thing to do to a person."

Now he began to snuffle piteously. I didn't know whether to take him into my arms and comfort him or kick him in the teeth. I did neither.

Finally, through his tears, he said, "I thought Barry would get off. I never thought he would be convicted. Really, Donald, I didn't!"

"How can you say that? You knew Thorne Cornwallis lacked both the guts and the fluency of mind to hold out for the truth. You were going to let him lock Barry away for life in some savage behavioral sink while you went off to a tropical isle and set up another jolly blowjobs-and-martinis hot-tub operation. Steven, I feel like puking myself."

"Oh, you're so sanctimonious, Donald! But you don't know. You just don't know."

"I don't know what?"

"What they said they would do to me!"

"What who said?"

Terror filled his eyes. "Michael. He told me if any of this ever got out, it would kill Anne Marie, and he would come after me wherever I was, and he would torture me like in Iraq with an electric drill. And I believe him. Jim always said Michael was a sadist with no class."

I seated myself on the edge of another chaise and looked down at Gaudios as he sat slumped and slobbering. I saw the silver band on his finger and asked, "When did you and Jim marry?"

He shook his head. "No. Oh no."

I said, "Ramona Furst will know in the morning when the state Division of Vital Statistics, Department of Public Health, opens. All marriages in the state are public records."

He began to weep again. After a moment, he croaked out, "It was last June twelfth. In Weston. We were married by a justice of the peace."

"Who was the witness?"

"A secretary in the office of the Weston town clerk on her lunch hour, Angie DiCello. She was so sweet. She said it was her first gay wedding, and she said she was proud to be part of history."

"Why Weston?"

"Because the town is quite elegant, and Jim and I both thought none of our relatives would ever look at the marriage records there. But a bitch in Pittsfield who's trying to get gay marriage overturned and spends her time snooping in the state registry saw our names there and told Michael. If anybody should be prosecuted, it should be her, fucking busybody Rosemary Mazzota."

"I'll mention her name to Thorny. But you know as well as I do who has to be prosecuted, Steven. It's the people who actually committed this crime, the people who took Jim away from you. And those people would be sadistic and sociopathic Michael Sturdivant and the vicious goon Cheap Maloney."

Gaudios just sat there staring up at me, smelling awful and trembling.

I said, "You have to tell the truth now, Steven. For Jim."

"No," he said, a little calmer now. "Jim wouldn't want me to tell the truth. You are entirely wrong about that."

"Why wouldn't he? After what they did to him?"

"No, if I told the truth, then Anne Marie would lose another son. One of her sons would be revealed as a murderer and the other one as a fag. Jim wouldn't want to hurt his mother that way, of that I am certain."

"Well, then," I said, "if you're not going to tell the truth for Jim, you're going to do it for Barry Fields."

He got teary again. "Right now? Do I have to do it right away?"

"No. Tomorrow is actually better. If you talked to the police today, it would be your word against Michael's. Tomorrow there should be additional evidence to be had." He looked at me quizzically but didn't pursue this. Gaudios had had enough of me for the moment.

I helped him into the house, where he could clean himself up and phone his friends, begging off on his luncheon engagement. He told them he was feeling somewhat unwell, and that was no social lie.

CHAPTER TWENTY-SEVEN

Our Lady of Mount Carmel Church was a handsome, well-cared-for red brick Romanesque building east of Pittsfield's downtown on Fenn Street near the post office. It had a religious education center attached on one side and a modest Eisenhower-era rectory across the street. The Astroturf on the church's front steps lacked Giotto-like grace but probably kept a lot of the older parishioners from breaking their necks.

The weather on Monday was cool and bright. When Timmy and I arrived at nine thirty, freshly waxed funeral cars were already dropping off mourners and then queuing down the street for the post-funeral-mass procession to the cemetery in Pittsfield's North End.

We parked on Third Street, which runs north off Fenn across from the church, in front of a row of dilapidated frame houses. David Murano had taken the day off from school and met us at the corner. He explained that this old Italian neighborhood had become more Hispanic in recent years, but that a lot of the old Italo-American families that had made money and moved to nicer neighborhoods still supported Mount Carmel.

For our purposes, the arrival of Reverend Felson and his gang was well-timed. The hearse carrying Jim Sturdivant's remains, to be followed by family members in limos, had not yet arrived at the church when the Felsons marched down Fenn past the post office, holding up their signs. There were eighteen or twenty in the flock, the reverend at the head of the ragtag column. A couple of the protesters couldn't have been older than twelve. The signs they waved were the famous ones we had seen in the news: *God Hates Fags. Homos Burn in Hell. Satan Loves Sodomy.* Most of the banners looked well worn, but two special signs had been created for this occasion: *Benjamin Krider Will Die of AIDS,* and *Jim Sturdivant Is Going to Homo Hell.*

The single Pittsfield uniformed police officer stationed in front of the church spotted the Felson gang, and as they approached him, he instructed them to move across the street to the rectory for their protest. This was not far from where Timmy, David and I stood. As shocked mourners entering the church either fell back and gawked in horror or, in a few cases, began groping for their cell phones, the reverend and his crew crossed Fenn and formed a circle in front of the rectory. They stood a few feet from us, beady-eyed and scowling, some of them muttering to others in their group, a few with their eyes squinched shut and apparently praying.

I walked over to a likely-looking couple in their late forties. The man had Barry Fields' radiant blue eyes, and the woman had his ample red lips. It was she who carried the sign that read *Benjamin Krider Will Die of AIDS*.

I said to them, "Your son is well. Or will be well as soon as you get out of town and let him live his good life."

The two stared at me as if Lucifer himself had ambled up to them on the sidewalk.

I said, "You'd be smart to leave here now. Really. Some bad people — people even worse than you are in their old-fashioned ways — are going to be plenty mad that you're here."

The woman yelled in my face, "The Lord your God is preparing to smite you!"

"I'll take my chances," I said.

"Are you a pervert?" the blue-eyed man demanded to know.

"Yeah, I am. Of course, now we say *gay*. Though younger people seem to prefer the more all-encompassing *queer* as a label. That term is looser than *gay* or *lesbian*, and also it has a defiant edge to it, owing to its origins as a brutal insult. Hey, who knows? Maybe *pervert* will be the next politically correct way we homos describe ourselves. And you'll go around screaming 'pervert! pervert!' and people will just respond, 'Hey, bro, gimme five!'"

The woman with hate in her eyes yelled, "This is a nation of perverts! Judgment is upon you! Massachusetts is in Satan's maw!"

Timmy and Murano had walked over and stood listening to this exchange, and Reverend Felson was headed our way too. I wondered if Timmy might attempt to engage the Felson–

Kriders in Socratic dialogue, an admirable habit of his in situations where conflicting opinions seem to have hardened hopelessly.

Instead, Timmy looked at the couple, and at Reverend Felson as he approached, and he said, "You morons would be smart to run for your lives. I'm not kidding either. You just don't know what this pervert here — that's Donald Strachey, the love of my life — you have no idea what this particular pervert has arranged for you."

The crowd in front of the church was growing now, with dozens of men in their funeral suits and ladies in their dark finery, and they glanced around nervously, apparently anticipating some type of intervention by the authorities. Some mourners were gesticulating to the cop, who seemed to be urging calm. Down the street, the workers at an auto-parts store had come outside to watch, and cars kept slowing down on busy Fenn Street so drivers could catch a glimpse of an unusual drama in the making.

Reverend Felson himself now addressed Timmy. He screeched, "The Lord is on the rampage! The fags are on the run!"

Timmy said, "Oh, I beg your pardon, pastor. Well, if this is the way you want it, what can I tell you?"

Just then the hearse pulled up in front of the church, followed by two limousines with flags, as if they carried the French ambassador and his chief of protocol. But the first man out of the head limo was no diplomat, for Murano said, "That's Michael."

Michael Sturdivant, both burly and sleek, quickly surveyed the scene, including the sign that read *Jim Sturdivant is Going to Homo Hell,* and yanked his cell phone out of the breast pocket of his well-cut black suit. He turned back toward the limo he had just exited, but by then a small lady in a lacy black dress and a hat with a veil had climbed out the other side of the car and was peering over at us and at Reverend Felson's gang. Michael spoke quickly into his phone and then went around and all but dragged his aged mother up the church steps and through the front door. The pallbearers had the casket out of the hearse now, and they headed for the Astroturfed steps, too, glancing our way and shooting us the evil eye from time to time, as they grunted and maneuvered.

Then the press arrived. Murano said, "Here comes the *Eagle*," as two young women trotted up the street, the one with the camera already snapping pictures.

The Felson gang, unembarrassed to illustrate the vanity of evil, posed for pictures eagerly, baring their fangs and hurling crude epithets at non-fundamentalists, at sodomites, and at the "media perverts" themselves.

The funeral was to start at ten, and we could see the cop across the street and a young priest ushering the gawkers into the church now. Some wished to linger, apparently, to see what would happen next, and who could blame them? They thought the show was far from over, and they were right.

At ten o'clock, the bell in Mount Carmel's tall brick tower tolled reverently, and soon after the church doors closed. The doors opened briefly a few minutes later, however, and Michael Sturdivant stepped outside and stood hulking on the top step. He glared over at the Felson gang and at Timmy and me. I thought, *He knows who we are.*

Sturdivant's cell phone must have rung, and he spoke into it and then peered off to the right, down Fenn Street past the auto-parts store. Two dark SUVs rounded a corner a block east of us. They moved quickly up Fenn and pulled over in front of the rectory. I recognized the New York state license plate on the second vehicle. Five men wielding baseball bats got out of the two SUVs and went after the Felsons. The reverend took a blow to his right shoulder and went down, and the Kriders raised their arms to absorb the blows, but they were hit too. I saw Michael Sturdivant crossing the street and pointing at Timmy, David and me, and I thought, *Where the hell are they?*

Then the door to the Mount Carmel rectory opened, and a combined Pittsfield and State Police SWAT team of thirty or more officers poured out, their guns drawn, and began subduing and cuffing the thugs. The vehicle with the New York tags still had a driver behind the wheel, and he made a break for it. But police vehicles had rapidly blocked both ends of Fenn, and Third Street, too, and the driver was soon out on the pavement, down and cuffed.

Michael Sturdivant had begun to back away from the melee, but Joe Toomey, who brought up the rear of the fast-moving SWAT team, spotted Sturdivant and directed two officers to bring him back and hold him, too. He sputtered with indignation, but Toomey ignored him.

It was Toomey who led the search of the two SUVs. He was there when the glove compartment of the Explorer from New York State yielded up a Glock-9 which was, it would soon be established, the gun that had killed Jim Sturdivant.

All this commotion brought some of the mourners out of the church and onto the sidewalk, and crowds were gathering up by the post office and outside the taverns farther down Fenn. Reverend Felson was lying on the sidewalk, moaning and clutching his shoulder, and others in his flock had been bloodied. The Felson children had not been hit, but they were crying and looked dazed. I could hear ambulances approaching from up Fenn Street.

Joe Toomey walked over to me. He said, "I talked to Thorny. He's releasing Barry Fields, withdrawing the charges. Myra Greene is in the clear, too."

"Never too late," I said.

"No, sometimes it is too late. But not in this case. Barry'll recover."

"What about this bunch?" I said, indicating the Felsons, as three ambulances cruised down Fenn and pulled in near us.

"What about them?" Toomey said.

"What can you charge them with? We've got to get them out of here if Barry is going to be able to stay in the Berkshires."

"I can't charge them with anything," Toomey said. "They're victims. As I think you can plainly see. In fact, they'll need to be around here to testify against the people who attacked them."

"Hell."

"Hey, you got the guys who killed Jim Sturdivant, and you cleared your client. What do you want? You can't have everything, Strachey. And I'll bet you're a strong believer in First Amendment rights, which these folks from the great American heartland were out here today exercising." Toomey looked at me with an expression I couldn't quite decipher.

As Michael Sturdivant and his marauders were carted off and the throngs of onlookers began to edge in closer for a glimpse of the lurid scene, I noticed an old priest walk out of the rectory, pick up the sign that read *Jim Sturdivant is Going to Homo Hell,* and carry the placard inside the building. I saw Timmy and David Murano take note of this, too. They came over, and Timmy said, "Old Pittsfield takes care of its own."

Murano just laughed.

Reverend Felson and his gang left town on their own and returned to Kansas, declaring Berkshire County irretrievably in Satan's grip. He declared to the *Eagle*, "You can smell the sulfur from Sheffield to Williamstown!" Cheap Maloney was convicted of murder, and Michael Sturdivant got forty years for conspiracy to commit murder. Thorne Cornwallis, who led the prosecution, was reelected in November with his usual seventy percent of the vote.

Steven Gaudios did testify against Michael and then went into the Witness Protection Program. He changed his name, and no one in the Berkshires ever knew where he went or what became of him. Jim Sturdivant was buried in his family's plot in St. Joseph's cemetery in Pittsfield. At trial, Thorny did not mention his brother's motive for having Jim rubbed out, and Michael wasn't about to bring it up, either. Michael was convicted on Steven's testimony and by Cheap Maloney's ratting him out.

In the *Eagle* story on the Mount Carmel anti-gay demonstration and mobster round-up, the *Jim Sturdivant is Going to Homo Hell* sign was mentioned. But all the people quoted in the story — Sturdivant family members, Mount Carmel parishioners, a priest — said they had no idea what that sign meant, and they said Reverend Felson must have had Jim mixed up with somebody else.

Barry Fields regained his freedom and his equilibrium but never entirely lost the anger and fear that came from his being a renegade from the Felsons. He remained in Great Barrington and married Bill Moore, who paid me my fee. Moore was flush, for I had suggested to Gaudios that decency required his canceling Moore's hot-tub debt, and he did so. Moore kept his FBI secret, and he stayed sad and drank a little too much. But he and Fields had each other, and that was quite a bit.

Timmy and I joined Murano, Morley, Ramona Furst, Bud Radziwill, Jean Watrous, and Barry and Bill six months later at

Myra Greene's retirement party. She looked around the room at one point and croaked, "This looks like the cast of *Casablanca*. I've never seen so many people with secrets in one place before. God, I can barely remember who's really who in here."

People laughed nervously, and then Fields said, "I think it's more like *Meet Me in St. Louis*, Myra — when the plans are canceled to move to New York, and the whole family gets to stay in St. Louis, and we know Judy's going to hop in the sack with Tom Drake."

"And marry him," Timmy added, and we all drank to that.

ABOUT THE AUTHOR

RICHARD STEVENSON is the pseudonym of Richard Lipez, the author of nine books, including the Don Strachey private eye series. The Strachey books are being filmed by here!, the first gay television network. Lipez also co-wrote Grand Scam with Peter Stein, and contributed to Crimes of the Scene: A Mystery Novel Guide for the International Traveler. He is a mystery columnist for The Washington Post and a former editorial writer at The Berkshire Eagle. His reporting, reviews and fiction have appeared in The Boston Globe, Newsday, The Progressive, The Atlantic Monthly, Harper's and many other publications. He grew up and went to college in Pennsylvania and served in the Peace Corps in Ethiopia from 1962-64. Lipez lives in Becket, Massachusetts and is married to sculptor Joe Wheaton.

Stimulate yourself.
READ.
www.manloveromance.com
THE HOTTEST M/M EROTIC AUTHORS & WEBSITES ON THE NET

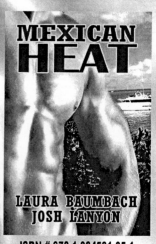